CONAN DOYLE
CENTENNIAL SERIES

Yours very truly
A Conan Doyle

THE DOINGS OF
RAFFLES HAW

A. Conan Doyle

Illustrations by
Paul M. McCall

Embellishments by
James B. Campbell

Afterword by
John Bennett Shaw

PUBLICATIONS

BLOOMINGTON, INDIANA   1981

The Doings of Raffles Haw
was originally published in December 1891
by J. H. Lovell Company (New York)
and in March 1892
by Cassell & Company (London)

This Edition Copyright © 1981 by Jack W. Tracy
All Rights Reserved

ISBN: 0-934468-43-5

Library of Congress
Catalogue Card No. 80-67702

Printed in the United States of America

First impression: December 1981

Second impression: March 1982

GASLIGHT PUBLICATIONS
112 East Second
Bloomington, Indiana 47401

To

MALCOLM MORRIS, ESQ., F.R.C.S.E.

OF 8, HARLEY STREET

CONTENTS

LIST OF ILLUSTRATIONS

THE DOINGS OF
RAFFLES HAW

"I wonder whether you could care for me if I were without a penny?"

A DOUBLE ENIGMA

"I'M AFRAID THAT HE WON'T COME," said Laura McIntyre, in a disconsolate voice.

"Why not?"

"Oh, look at the weather; it is something too awful."

As she spoke a whirl of snow beat with a muffled patter against the cosy red-curtained window, while a long blast of wind shrieked and whistled through the branches of the great white-limbed elms which skirted the garden.

Robert McIntyre rose from the sketch upon which he had been working, and taking one of the lamps in his hand peered out into the darkness. The long skeleton limbs of the bare trees tossed and quivered dimly amid the whirling drift. His sister sat by the fire, her fancy-work in her lap, and looked up at her brother's profile which showed against the brilliant yellow light. It was a handsome face, young and fair and clear cut, with wavy brown hair combed backwards and rippling down into that outward curve at the ends which one associates with the artistic temperament. There was refinement too in his slightly puckered eyes, his dainty gold-rimmed *pince-nez* glasses, and in the black velveteen coat which caught the light so richly upon its shoulder. In his mouth only there was something — a suspicion of

3

coarseness, a possibility of weakness — which in the eyes of some, and of his sister among them, marred the grace and beauty of his features. Yet, as he was wont himself to say, when one thinks that each poor mortal is heir to a legacy of every evil trait or bodily taint of so vast a line of ancestors, lucky indeed is the man who does not find that Nature has scored up some long-owing family debt upon his features.

And indeed in this case the remorseless creditor had gone so far as to exact a claim from the lady also, though in her case the extreme beauty of the upper part of the face drew the eye away from any weakness which might be found in the lower. She was darker than her brother — so dark that her heavily coiled hair seemed to be black until the light shone slantwise across it. The delicate, half-petulant features, the finely traced brows, and the thoughtful, humorous eyes were all perfect in their way, and yet the combination left something to be desired. There was a vague sense of a flaw somewhere, in feature or in expression, which resolved itself, when analyzed, into a slight out-turning and droop of the lower lip; small indeed, and yet pronounced enough to turn what would have been a beautiful face into a merely pretty one. Very despondent and somewhat cross she looked as she leaned back in the armchair, the tangle of bright-coloured silks and of drab holland upon her lap, her hands clasped behind her head, with her snowy forearms and little pink elbows projecting on either side.

"I know he won't come," she repeated.

"Nonsense, Laura! Of course he'll come. A sailor and afraid of the weather!"

"Ha!" She raised her finger, and a smile of triumph played over her face, only to die away again into a blank look of disappointment. "It is only papa," she murmured.

A shuffling step was heard in the hall, and a little peaky man, with slippers very much down at the heels, came shambling into the room. Mr. McIntyre, sen., was pale and furtive-looking, with a thin straggling red beard shot with grey, and a sunken downcast face. Ill-fortune and ill-health had both left their marks upon him. Ten years before he had been one of the largest and richest gunmakers in Birmingham, but a long run of commercial bad luck had sapped his great fortune, and had finally driven him into the Bankruptcy Court. The death of his wife on the very day of his insolvency had filled his cup of sorrow, and he had gone about since with a stunned, half-dazed expression upon his weak pallid face which spoke of a mind unhinged. So complete had been his downfall that the family would have been reduced to absolute poverty were it not for a small legacy of two-hundred a year which both the children had received from one of their uncles upon the mother's side who had amassed a fortune in Australia. By combining their incomes, and by taking a house in the quiet country district of Tamfield, some fourteen miles from the great Midland city, they were still able to live with some approach to comfort. The change, however, was a bitter one to all — to Robert, who had to forego the luxuries dear to his artistic temperament, and to think of turning what had been merely an over-ruling hobby into a means of earning a living; and even more to Laura, who winced before the pity of her old friends, and found the lanes and fields of Tamfield intolerably dull after the life and bustle of Edgbaston. Their discomfort was aggravated by the conduct of their father, whose life now was one long wail over his misfortunes, and who alternately sought comfort in the Prayer-book and in the decanter for the ills which had befallen him.

To Laura, however, Tamfield presented one attraction, which was now about to be taken from her. Their choice of the little country hamlet as their residence had been determined by the fact of their old friend, the Reverend John Spurling, having been nominated as the vicar. Hector Spurling, the elder son, two months Laura's senior, had been engaged to her for some years, and was, indeed, upon the point of marrying her when the sudden financial crash had disarranged their plans. A sub-lieutenant in the Navy, he was home on leave at present, and hardly an evening passed without his making his way from the Vicarage to Elmdene, where the McIntyres resided. To-day, however, a note had reached them to the effect that he had been suddenly ordered on duty, and that he must rejoin his ship at Portsmouth by the next evening. He would look in, were it but for half-an-hour, to bid them adieu.

"Why, where's Hector?" asked Mr. McIntyre, blinking round from side to side.

"He's not come, father. How could you expect him to come on such a night as this? Why, there must be two feet of snow in the glebe field."

"Not come, eh?" croaked the old man, throwing himself down upon the sofa. "Well, well, it only wants him and his father to throw us over, and the thing will be complete."

"How can you even hint at such a thing, father?" cried Laura indignantly. "They have been as true as steel. What would they think if they heard you?"

"I think, Robert," he said, disregarding his daughter's protest, "that I will have a drop, just the very smallest possible drop, of brandy. A mere thimbleful will do; but I rather think I have caught cold during the snowstorm to-day."

Robert went on sketching stolidly in his folding book, but Laura looked up from her work.

"I'm afraid there is nothing in the house, father," she said.

"Laura! Laura!" He shook his head as one more in sorrow than in anger. "You are no longer a girl, Laura; you are a woman, the manager of a household, Laura. We trust in you. We look entirely towards you. And yet you leave your poor brother Robert without any brandy, to say nothing of me, your father. Good heavens, Laura! what would your mother have said? Think of accidents, think of sudden illness, think of apoplectic fits, Laura. It is a very grave res — a very grave respons — a very great risk that you run."

"I hardly touch the stuff," said Robert curtly; "Laura need not provide any for me."

"As a medicine it is invaluable, Robert. To be used, you understand, and not to be abused. That's the whole secret of it. But I'll step down to the Three Pigeons for half an hour."

"My dear father," cried the young man, "you surely are not going out upon such a night. If you must have brandy could I not send Sarah for some? Please let me send Sarah; or I would go myself, or — "

Pip! came a little paper pellet from his sister's chair on to the sketch-book in front of him! He unrolled it and held it to the light.

"For Heaven's sake let him go!" was scrawled across it.

"Well, in any case, wrap yourself up warm," he continued, laying bare his sudden change of front with

a masculine clumsiness which horrified his sister.
"Perhaps it is not so cold as it looks. You can't lose your
way, that is one blessing. And it is not more than a
hundred yards."

With many mumbles and grumbles at his daughter's
want of foresight, old McIntyre struggled into his
great-coat and wrapped his scarf round his long thin
throat. A sharp gust of cold wind made the lamps
flicker as he threw open the hall-door. His two children
listened to the dull fall of his footsteps as he slowly
picked out the winding garden path.

"He gets worse — he becomes intolerable," said
Robert at last. "We should not have let him out; he
may make a public exhibition of himself."

"But it's Hector's last night," pleaded Laura. "It
would be dreadful if they met and he noticed anything.
That was why I wished him to go."

"Then you were only just in time," remarked her
brother, "for I hear the gate go, and — yes, you see."

As he spoke a cheery hail came from outside, with a
sharp rat-tat at the window. Robert stepped out and
threw open the door to admit a tall young man, whose
black frieze jacket was all mottled and glistening with
snow crystals. Laughing loudly he shook himself like a
Newfoundland dog, and kicked the snow from his boots
before entering the little lamplit room.

Hector Spurling's profession was written in every
line of his face. The clean-shaven lip and chin, the little
fringe of side whisker, the straight decisive mouth, and
the hard weather-tanned cheeks all spoke of the Royal
Navy. Fifty such faces may be seen any night of the
year round the mess-table of the Royal Naval College
in Portsmouth Dockyard — faces which bear a closer
resemblance to each other than brother does commonly

to brother. They are all cast in a common mould, the products of a system which teaches early self-reliance, hardihood, and manliness — a fine type upon the whole; less refined and less intellectual, perhaps, than their brothers of the land, but full of truth and energy and heroism. In figure he was straight, tall, and well-knit, with keen grey eyes, and the sharp prompt manner of a man who has been accustomed both to command and to obey.

"You had my note?" he said, as he entered the room. "I have to go again, Laura. Isn't it a bore? Old Smithers is short-handed, and wants me back at once." He sat down by the girl, and put his brown hand across her white one. "It won't be a very large order this time," he continued. "It's the flying squadron business — Madeira, Gibraltar, Lisbon, and home. I shouldn't wonder if we were back in March."

"It seems only the other day that you landed," she answered.

"Poor little girl! But it won't be long. Mind you take good care of her, Robert, when I am gone. And when I come again, Laura, it will be the last time mind! Hang the money! There are plenty who manage on less. We need not have a house. Why should we? You can get very nice rooms in Southsea at £2 a week. McDougall, our paymaster, has just married, and he only gives thirty shillings. You would not be afraid, Laura?"

"No, indeed."

"The dear old governor is so awfully cautious. Wait, wait, wait, that's always his cry. I tell him that he ought to have been in the Government Heavy Ordnance Department. But I'll speak to him to-night. I'll talk him round. See if I don't. And you must speak to your own governor. Robert here will back you up. And here are the ports and the dates that we are due at each. Mind that you have a letter waiting for me at every one."

He took a slip of paper from the side pocket of his coat, but, instead of handing it to the young lady, he remained staring at it with the utmost astonishment upon his face.

"Well, I never!" he exclaimed. "Look here, Robert; what do you call this?"

"Hold it to the light. Why, it's a fifty-pound Bank of England note. Nothing remarkable about it that I can see."

"On the contrary. It's the queerest thing that ever happened to me. I can't make head or tail of it."

"Come, then, Hector," cried Miss McIntyre with a challenge in her eyes. "Something very queer happened to me also to-day. I'll bet a pair of gloves that my adventure was more out of the common than yours, though I have nothing so nice to show at the end of it."

"Come, I'll take that, and Robert here shall be the judge."

"State your cases." The young artist shut up his sketch-book, and rested his head upon his hands with a face of mock solemnity. "Ladies first! Go along, Laura, though I think I know something of your adventure already."

"It was this morning, Hector," she said. "Oh, by the way, the story will make you wild. I had forgotten that. However, you mustn't mind, because, really, the poor fellow was perfectly mad."

"What on earth was it?" asked the young officer, his eyes travelling from the bank-note to his *fiancée*.

"Oh, it was harmless enough, and yet you will confess it was very queer. I had gone out for a walk, but as the snow began to fall I took shelter under the shed

which the workmen have built at the near end of the
great new house. The men have gone, you know, and
the owner is supposed to be coming to-morrow, but the
shed is still standing. I was sitting there upon a packing-
case when a man came down the road and stopped
under the same shelter. He was a quiet, pale-faced
man, very tall and thin, not much more than thirty, I
should think, poorly dressed, but with the look and
bearing of a gentleman. He asked me one or two
questions about the village and the people, which, of
course, I answered, until at last we found ourselves
chatting away in the pleasantest and easiest fashion
about all sorts of things. The time passed so quickly
that I forgot all about the snow until he drew my
attention to its having stopped for the moment. Then,
just as I was turning to go, what in the world do you
suppose that he did? He took a step towards me, looked
in a sad pensive way into my face, and said: 'I wonder
whether you could care for me if I were without a
penny.' Wasn't it strange? I was so frightened that I
whisked out of the shed, and was off down the road
before he could add another word. But really, Hector,
you need not look so black, for when I look back at it I
can quite see from his tone and manner that he meant
no harm. He was thinking aloud, without the least
intention of being offensive. I am convinced that the
poor fellow was mad."

"Hum! There was some method in his madness, it
seems to me," remarked her brother.

"There would have been some method in my
kicking," said the lieutenant savagely. "I never heard
of a more outrageous thing in my life."

"Now, I said that you would be wild!" She laid her
white hand upon the sleeve of his rough frieze jacket.

"It was nothing. I shall never see the poor fellow again. He was evidently a stranger to this part of the country. But that was my little adventure. Now let us have yours."

The man crackled the bank-note between his fingers and thumb, while he passed his other hand over his hair with the action of a man who strives to collect himself.

"It is some ridiculous mistake," he said. "I must try and set it right. Yet I don't know how to set about it either. I was going down to the village from the Vicarage just after dusk when I found a fellow in a trap who had got himself into broken water. One wheel had sunk into the edge of the ditch which had been hidden by the snow, and the whole thing was high and dry, with a list to starboard enough to slide him out of his seat. I lent a hand, of course, and soon had the wheel in the road again. It was quite dark, and I fancy that the fellow thought that I was a bumpkin, for we did not exchange five words. As he drove off he shoved this into my hand. It is the merest chance that I did not chuck it away, for, feeling that it was a crumpled piece of paper, I imagined that it must be a tradesman's advertisement or something of the kind. However, as luck would have it, I put it in my pocket, and there I found it when I looked for the dates of our cruise. Now you know as much of the matter as I do."

Brother and sister stared at the black and white crinkled note with astonishment upon their faces.

"Why, your unknown traveller must have been Monte Cristo, or Rothschild at the least!" said Robert. "I am bound to say, Laura, that I think you have lost your bet."

"Oh, I am quite content to lose it. I never heard of

such a piece of luck. What a perfectly delightful man this must be to know."

"But I can't take his money," said Hector Spurling, looking somewhat ruefully at the note. "A little prize-money is all very well in its way, but a Johnny must draw the line somewhere. Besides it must have been a mistake. And yet he meant to give me something big, for he could not mistake a note for a coin. I suppose I must advertise for the fellow."

"It seems a pity, too," remarked Robert. "I must say that I don't quite see it in the same light that you do."

"Indeed I think that you are very Quixotic, Hector," said Laura McIntyre. "Why should you not accept it in the spirit in which it was meant? You did this stranger a service — perhaps a greater service than you know of — and he meant this as a little memento of the occasion. I do not see that there is any possible reason against your keeping it."

"Oh, come!" said the young sailor, with an embarrassed laugh, "it is not quite the thing — not the sort of story one would care to tell at mess."

"In any case you are off to-morrow morning," observed Robert. "You have no time to make inquiries about the mysterious Crœsus. You must really make the best of it."

"Well, look here, Laura, you put it in your work-basket," cried Hector Spurling. "You shall be my banker, and if the rightful owner turns up then I can refer him to you. If not, I suppose we must look on it as a kind of salvage-money, though I am bound to say I don't feel entirely comfortable about it." He rose to his feet, and threw the note down into the brown basket of coloured wools which stood beside her. "Now, Laura, I must up anchor, for I promised the governor to be back by nine. It won't be long this time, dear, and it shall be the last. Good-bye, Robert! Good luck!"

"Good-bye, Hector! *Bon voyage!*" The young artist remained by the table, while his sister followed her lover to the door. In the dim light of the hall he could see their figures and overhear their words.

"Next time, little girl?"

"Next time be it, Hector."

"And nothing can part us?"

"Nothing."

"In the whole world?"

"Nothing."

Robert discreetly closed the door. A moment later a thud from without, and the quick footsteps crunching on the snow told him that their visitor had departed.

II

The Tenant of the New Hall

T HE SNOW had ceased to fall, but for a week a hard frost had held the country side in its iron grip. The roads rang under the horses' hoofs, and every wayside ditch and runlet was a street of ice. Over the long undulating landscape the red brick houses peeped out warmly against the spotless background, and the lines of grey smoke streamed straight up into the windless air. The sky was of the lightest pale blue, and the morning sun, shining through the distant fog-wreaths of Birmingham, struck a subdued glow from the broad-spread snowfields which might have gladdened the eyes of an artist.

It did gladden the heart of one who viewed it that morning from the summit of the gently-curving Tamfield Hill. Robert McIntyre stood with his elbows upon a gate-rail, his Tam-o'-Shanter hat over his eyes, and a short briar-root pipe in his mouth, looking slowly about him, with the absorbed air of one who breathes his fill of Nature. Beneath him to the north lay the village of Tamfield, red walls, grey roofs, and a scattered bristle of dark trees, with his own little Elmdene nestling back from the broad, white winding Birmingham Road. At the other side, as he slowly faced round, lay a vast stone building, white and clear-

cut, fresh from the builders' hands. A great tower shot
up from one corner of it, and a hundred windows
twinkled ruddily in the light of the morning sun. A little
distance from it stood a second small square low-lying
structure, with a tall chimney rising from the midst of
it, rolling out a long plume of smoke into the frosty air.
The whole vast structure stood within its own grounds,
enclosed by a stately park wall, and surrounded by
what would in time be an extensive plantation of fir-
trees. By the lodge gates a vast pile of *débris,* with lines
of sheds for workmen, and huge heaps of planks from
scaffoldings, all proclaimed that the work had only just
been brought to an end.

Robert McIntyre looked down with curious eyes at
the broad-spread building. It had long been a mystery
and a subject of gossip for the whole country side.
Hardly a year had elapsed since the rumour had first
gone about that a millionaire had bought a tract of
land, and that it was his intention to build a country
seat upon it. Since then the work had been pushed on
night and day, until now it was finished to the last
detail in a shorter time than it takes to build many a
six-roomed cottage. Every morning two long special
trains had arrived from Birmingham, carrying down a
great army of labourers, who were relieved in the
evening by a fresh gang, who carried on their task
under the rays of twelve enormous electric lights. The
number of workmen appeared to be only limited by the
space into which they could be fitted. Great lines of
waggons conveyed the white Portland stone from the
depôt by the station. Hundreds of busy toilers handed
it over, shaped and squared, to the actual masons, who
swung it up with steam cranes on to the growing walls,
where it was instantly fitted and mortared by their

companions. Day by day the house shot higher, while pillar and cornice and carving seemed to bud out from it as if by magic. Nor was the work confined to the main building. A large separate structure sprang up at the same time, and there came gangs of pale-faced men from London with much extraordinary machinery, vast cylinders, wheels and wires, which they fitted up in this outlying building. The great chimney which rose from the centre of it, combined with these strange furnishings, seemed to mean that it was reserved as a factory or place of business, for it was rumoured that this rich man's hobby was the same as a poor man's necessity, and that he was fond of working with his own hands amid chemicals and furnaces. Scarce, too, was the second storey begun ere the wood-workers and plumbers and furnishers were busy beneath, carrying out a thousand strange and costly schemes for the greater comfort and convenience of the owner. Singular stories were told all round the country, and even in Birmingham itself, of the extraordinary luxury and the absolute disregard for money which marked all these arrangements. No sum appeared to be too great to spend upon the smallest detail which might do away with or lessen any of the petty inconveniences of life. Waggons and waggons of the richest furniture had passed through the village between lines of staring villagers. Costly skins, glossy carpets, rich rugs, ivory, and ebony, and metal; every glimpse into these store-houses of treasure had given rise to some new legend. And finally, when all had been arranged, there had come a staff of forty servants, who heralded the approach of the owner, Mr. Raffles Haw himself.

It was no wonder, then, that it was with considerable curiosity that Robert McIntyre looked down at the great house, and marked the smoking chimneys, the curtained windows, and the other signs which showed that its tenant had arrived. A vast area of greenhouses gleamed like a lake on the further side, and beyond were the long lines of stables and outhouses. Fifty horses had passed through Tamfield the week before, so that, large as were the preparations, they were not more than would be needed. Who and what could this man be who spent his money with so lavish a hand? His name was unknown. Birmingham was as ignorant as Tamfield as to his origin or the sources of his wealth. Robert McIntyre brooded languidly over the problem as he leaned against the gate, puffing his blue clouds of bird's-eye into the crisp, still air.

Suddenly his eye caught a dark figure emerging from the Avenue gates and striding up the winding road. A few minutes brought him near enough to show a familiar face looking over the stiff collar and from under the soft black hat of an English clergyman.

"Good-morning, Mr. Spurling."

"Ah, good-morning, Robert. How are you? Are you coming my way? How slippery the roads are!"

His round, kindly face was beaming with good nature, and he took little jumps as he walked, like a man who can hardly contain himself for pleasure.

"Have you heard from Hector?"

"Oh, yes. He went off all right last Wednesday from Spithead, and he will write from Madeira. But you generally have later news at Elmdene than I have."

"I don't know whether Laura has heard. Have you been up to see the new comer?"

"Yes; I have just left him."

"Is he a married man — this Mr. Raffles Haw?"

"No, he is a bachelor. He does not seem to have any

relations either, as far as I could learn. He lives alone, amid his huge staff of servants. It is a most remarkable establishment. It made me think of the Arabian Nights."

"And the man? What is he like?"

"He is an angel — a positive angel. I never heard or read of such kindness in my life. He has made me a happy man."

The clergyman's eyes sparkled with emotion, and he blew his nose loudly in his big red handkerchief.

Robert McIntyre looked at him in surprise.

"I am delighted to hear it," he said. "May I ask what he has done?"

"I went up to him by appointment this morning. I had written asking him if I might call. I spoke to him of the parish and its needs, of my long struggle to restore the south side of the church, and of our efforts to help my poor parishioners during this hard weather. While I spoke he said not a word, but sat with a vacant face, as though he were not listening to me. When I had finished he took up his pen. 'How much will it take to do the church?' he asked. 'A thousand pounds,' I answered; 'but we have already raised three hundred among ourselves. The Squire has very handsomely given fifty pounds.' 'Well,' said he, 'how about the poor folk? How many families are there?' 'About three hundred,' I answered. 'And coals, I believe, are at about a pound a ton,' said he. 'Three tons ought to see them through the rest of the winter. Then you can get a very fair pair of blankets for two pounds. That would make five pounds per family, and seven hundred for the church.' He dipped his pen in the ink, and, as I am a living man, Robert, he wrote me a cheque then and there for two thousand two hundred pounds. I don't know what I said; I felt like a fool; I could not stammer out words with which to thank him. All my troubles have been taken from my shoulders in an instant, and indeed, Robert, I can hardly realize it."

"He must be a most charitable man."

"Extraordinarily so. And so unpretending. One would think that it was I who was doing the favour and he who was the beggar. I thought of that passage about making the heart of the widow sing for joy. He made my heart sing for joy, I can tell you. Are you coming up to the Vicarage?"

"No, thank you, Mr. Spurling. I must go home and get to work on my new picture. It's a five-foot canvas — the landing of the Romans in Kent. I must have another try for the Academy. Good-morning."

He raised his hat and continued down the road, while the vicar turned off into the path which led to his home.

Robert McIntyre had converted a large bare room in the upper storey of Elmdene into a studio, and thither he retreated after lunch. It was as well that he should have some little den of his own, for his father would talk of little save of his ledgers and accounts, while Laura had become peevish and querulous since the one tie which held her to Tamfield had been removed. The chamber was a bare and bleak one, unpapered and uncarpeted, but a good fire sparkled in the grate, and two large windows gave him the needful light. His easel stood in the centre, with the great canvas balanced across it, while against the walls there leaned his two last attempts, "The Murder of Thomas of Canterbury" and "The Signing of Magna Charta." Robert had a weakness for large subjects and broad effects. If his ambition was greater than his skill, he had still all the love of his art and the patience under discouragement which are the stuff out of which successful painters are made. Twice his brace of pictures had journeyed to town, and twice they had come back to him, until the finely gilded frames which had made such a call upon his purse began to show signs of these varied adventures. Yet, in spite of their depressing company, Robert turned to his fresh work with all the enthusiasm which a conviction of ultimate success can inspire.

But he could not work that afternoon. In vain he dashed in his background and outlined the long curves of the Roman galleys. Do what he would, his mind would still wander from his work to dwell upon his conversation with the vicar in the morning. His imagination was fascinated by the idea of this strange man living alone amid a crowd, and yet wielding such a power that with one dash of his pen he could change sorrow into joy, and transform the condition of a whole parish. The incident of the fifty-pound note came back to his mind. It must surely have been Raffles Haw with whom Hector Spurling had come in contact. There could not be two men in one parish to whom so large a sum was of so small an account as to be thrown to a bystander in return for a trifling piece of assistance. Of course, it must have been Raffles Haw. And his sister had the note, with instructions to return it to the owner, could he be found. He threw aside his palette, and descending into the sitting-room he told Laura and his father of his morning's interview with the vicar, and of his conviction that this was the man of whom Hector was in quest.

"Tut! tut!" said old McIntyre. "How is this, Laura? I knew nothing of this. What do women know of money or of business? Hand the note over to me and I shall relieve you of all responsibility. I will take everything upon myself."

"I cannot possibly, papa," said Laura, with decision. "I should not think of parting with it."

"What is the world coming to?" cried the old man, with his thin hands held up in protest. "You grow more undutiful every day, Laura. This money would be of use to me — of use, you understand. It may be the corner-stone of the vast business which I shall reconstruct. I will use it, Laura, and I will pay something — four, shall we say, or even four and a-half — and you may have it back on any day. And I will give security — the security of my — well, of my word of honour."

"It is quite impossible, papa," his daughter answered coldly. "It is not my money. Hector asked me to be his banker. Those were his very words. It is not in my power to lend it. As to what you say, Robert, you may be right or you may be wrong, but I certainly shall not give Mr. Raffles Haw or anyone else the money without Hector's express command."

"You are very right about not giving it to Mr. Raffles Haw," cried old McIntyre, with many nods of approbation. "I should certainly not let it go out of the family."

"Well, I thought that I would tell you."

Robert picked up his Tam-o'-Shanter and strolled out to avoid the discussion between his father and sister, which he saw was about to be renewed. His artistic nature revolted at these petty and sordid disputes, and he turned to the crisp air and the broad landscape to soothe his ruffled feelings. Avarice had no place among his failings, and his father's perpetual chatter about money inspired him with a positive loathing and disgust for the subject.

Robert was lounging slowly along his favourite walk which curled over the hill, with his mind turning from the Roman invasion to the mysterious millionaire, when his eyes fell upon a tall, lean man in front of him, who, with a pipe between his lips, was endeavouring to light a match under cover of his cap. The man was clad in a rough pea-jacket, and bore traces of smoke and grime upon his face and hands. Yet there is a Freemasonry among smokers which overrides every social difference, so Robert stopped and held out his case of fusees.

"A light?" said he.

"Thank you." The man picked out a fusee, struck it, and bent his head to it. He had a pale, thin face, a short straggling beard, and a very sharp and curving nose, with decision and character in the straight thick eyebrows which almost met on either side of it. Clearly a superior kind of workman, and possibly one of those who had been employed in the construction of the new house. Here was a chance of getting some first-hand information on the question which had aroused his curiosity. Robert waited until he had lit his pipe, and then walked on beside him.

"Are you going in the direction of the new Hall?" he asked.

"Yes."

The man's voice was cold, and his manner reserved.

"Perhaps you were engaged in the building of it?"

"Yes, I had a hand in it."

"They say that it is a wonderful place inside. It has been quite the talk of the district. Is it as rich as they say?"

"I am sure I don't know. I have not heard what they say."

His attitude was certainly not encouraging, and it seemed to Robert that he gave little sidelong suspicious glances at him out of his keen grey eyes. Yet, if he were so careful and discreet there was the more reason to think that there was information to be extracted, if he could but find a way to it.

"Ah, there it lies!" he remarked, as they topped the brow of the hill, and looked down once more at the great building. "Well, no doubt it is very gorgeous and splendid, but really for my own part I would rather live in my own little box down yonder in the village."

The workman puffed gravely at his pipe.

"You are no great admirer of wealth, then?" he said.

"Not I. I should not care to be a penny richer than I am. Of course I should like to sell my pictures. One must make a living. But beyond that I ask nothing. I dare say that I, a poor artist, or you, a man who work for your bread, have more happiness out of life than the owner of that great palace."

"Indeed, I think that it is more than likely," the other answered, in a much more conciliatory voice.

"Art," said Robert, warming to the subject, "is her own reward. What mere bodily indulgence is there which money could buy which can give that deep thrill of satisfaction which comes on the man who has conceived something new, something beautiful, and the daily delight as he sees it grow under his hand, until it stands before him a completed whole? With my art and without wealth I am happy. Without my art I should have a void which no money could fill. But I really don't know why I should say all this to you."

The workman had stopped, and was staring at him earnestly with a look of the deepest interest upon his smoke-darkened features.

"I am very glad to hear what you say," said he. "It is a pleasure to know that the worship of gold is not quite universal, and that there are at least some who can rise above it. Would you mind my shaking you by the hand?"

It was a somewhat extraordinary request, but Robert rather prided himself upon his Bohemianism, and upon his happy facility for making friends with all sorts and conditions of men. He readily exchanged a cordial grip with the chance acquaintance.

"You expressed some curiosity as to this house. I know the grounds pretty well, and might perhaps show you one or two little things which would interest you. Here are the gates. Will you come in with me?"

Here was, indeed, a chance. Robert eagerly assented, and walked up the winding drive amid the growing fir-trees. When he found his uncouth guide, however, marching straight across the broad, gravel square to the main entrance, he felt that he had placed himself in a false position.

"Surely not through the front door," he whispered, plucking his companion by the sleeve. "Perhaps Mr. Raffles Haw might not like it."

"I don't think there will be any difficulty," said the other, with a quiet smile. "My name is Raffles Haw."

"It's taken from the Alhambra," said Raffles Haw.

III

A House of Wonders

ROBERT McINTYRE'S FACE must have expressed the utter astonishment which filled his mind at this most unlooked-for announcement. For a moment he thought that his companion must be joking, but the ease and assurance with which he lounged up the steps, and the deep respect with which a richly-clad functionary in the hall swung open the door to admit him, showed that he spoke in sober earnest. Raffles Haw glanced back, and seeing the look of absolute amazement upon the young artist's features, he chuckled quietly to himself.

"You will forgive me, won't you, for not disclosing my identity?" he said, laying his hand with a friendly gesture upon the other's sleeve. "Had you known me you would have spoken less freely, and I should not have had the opportunity of learning your true worth. For example, you might hardly have been so frank upon the matter of wealth had you known that you were speaking to the master of the Hall."

"I don't think that I was ever so astonished in my life," gasped Robert.

"Naturally you are. How could you take me for anything but a workman? So I am. Chemistry is one of my hobbies, and I spend hours a day in my laboratory yonder. I have only just struck work, and as I had inhaled some not-over-pleasant gases, I thought that a turn down the road and a whiff of tobacco might do me good. That was how I came to meet you, and my toilet, I fear, corresponded only too well with my smoke-grimed face. But I rather fancy I know you by repute. Your name is Robert McIntyre, is it not?"

"Yes, though I cannot imagine how you knew."

"Well, I naturally took some little trouble to learn something of my neighbours. I had heard that there was an artist of that name, and I presume that artists are not very numerous in Tamfield. But how do you like the design? I hope it does not offend your trained taste."

"Indeed, it is wonderful — marvellous! You must yourself have an extraordinary eye for effect."

"Oh, I have no taste at all; not the slightest. I cannot tell good from bad. There never was such a complete Philistine. But I had the best man in London down, and another fellow from Vienna. They fixed it up between them."

They had been standing just within the folding doors upon a huge mat of bison skins. In front of them lay a great square court, paved with many-coloured marbles laid out in a labyrinth of arabesque design. In the centre a high fountain of carved jade shot five thin feathers of spray into the air, four of which curved towards each corner of the court to descend into broad marble basins, while the fifth mounted straight up to an immense height, and then trickled back into the central reservoir. On either side of the court a tall, graceful palm-tree shot up its slender stem to break into a crown of drooping green leaves some fifty feet above their heads. All round were a series of Moorish arches, in

jade and serpentine marble, with heavy curtains of the
deepest purple to cover the doors which lay between
them. In front, to right and to left, a broad staircase of
marble, carpeted with rich thick Smyrna rug work, led
upwards to the upper storeys, which were arranged
around the central court. The temperature within was
warm and yet fresh, like the air of an English May.

"It's taken from the Alhambra," said Raffles Haw.
"The palm-trees are pretty. They strike right through
the building into the ground beneath, and their roots
are all girt round with hot-water pipes. They seem to
thrive very well."

"What beautifully delicate brass-work!" cried
Robert, looking up with admiring eyes at the bright
and infinitely fragile metal trellis screens which adorned
the spaces between the Moorish arches.

"It is rather neat. But it is not brass-work. Brass is
not tough enough to allow them to work it to that
degree of fineness. It is gold. But just come this way
with me. You won't mind waiting while I remove this
smoke?"

He led the way to a door upon the left side of the
court, which, to Robert's surprise, swung slowly open
as they approached it.

"That is a little improvement which I have adopted,"
remarked the master of the house. "As you go up to a
door your weight upon the planks releases a spring
which causes the hinges to revolve. Pray step in. This is
my own little sanctum, and furnished after my own
heart."

If Robert expected to see some fresh exhibition of
wealth and luxury he was wofully disappointed, for he
found himself in a large but bare room, with a little
iron truckle-bed in one corner, a few scattered wooden

chairs, a dingy carpet, and a large table heaped with books, bottles, papers, and all the other *débris* which collect around a busy and untidy man. Motioning his visitor into a chair, Raffles Haw pulled off his coat, and, turning up the sleeves of his coarse flannel shirt, he began to plunge and scrub in the warm water which flowed from a tap in the wall.

"You see how simple my own tastes are," he remarked, as he mopped his dripping face and hair with the towel. "This is the only room in my great house where I find myself in a congenial atmosphere. It is homely to me. I can read here and smoke my pipe in peace. Anything like luxury is abhorrent to me."

"Really, I should not have thought it," observed Robert.

"It is a fact, I assure you. You see, even with your views as to the worthlessness of wealth, views which, I am sure, are very sensible and much to your credit, you must allow that if a man should happen to be the possessor of vast — well, let us say of considerable — sums of money, it is his duty to get that money into circulation, so that the community may be the better for it. There is the secret of my fine feathers. I have to exert all my ingenuity in order to spend my income, and yet to keep the money in legitimate channels. For example, it is very easy to give money away, and no doubt I could dispose of my surplus, or part of my surplus, in that fashion, but I have no wish to pauperize anyone, or to do mischief by indiscriminate charity. I must exact some sort of money's worth for all the money which I lay out. You see my point, don't you?"

"Entirely; though really it is something novel to hear a man complain of the difficulty of spending his income."

"I assure you that it is a very serious difficulty with me. But I have hit upon some plans — some very pretty plans. Will you wash your hands? Well, then, perhaps you would care to have a look round. Just come into this corner of the room, and sit upon this chair. So. Now I will sit upon this one, and we are ready to start."

The angle of the chamber in which they sat was painted for about six feet in each direction of a dark chocolate-brown, and was furnished with two red plush seats protruding from the walls, and in striking contrast with the simplicity of the rest of the apartment.

"This," remarked Raffles Haw, "is a lift, though it is so closely joined to the rest of the room that without the change in colour it might puzzle you to find the division. It is made to run either horizontally or vertically. This line of knobs represents the various rooms. You can see 'Dining,' 'Smoking,' 'Billiard,' 'Library,' and so on, upon them. I will show you the upward action. I press this one with 'Kitchen' upon it."

There was a sense of motion, a very slight jar, and Robert, without moving from his seat, was conscious that the room had vanished, and that a large arched oaken door stood in the place which it had occupied.

"That is the kitchen door," said Raffles Haw. "I have my kitchen at the top of the house. I cannot tolerate the smell of cooking. We have come up eighty feet in a very few seconds. Now I press again and here we are in my room once more."

Robert McIntyre stared about him in astonishment.

"The wonders of science are greater than those of magic," he remarked.

"Yes, it is a pretty little mechanism. Now we try the horizontal. I press the 'Dining' knob and here we are, you see. Step towards the door, and you will find it open in front of you."

Robert did as he was bid, and found himself with his companion in a large and lofty room, while the lift, the instant that it was freed from their weight, flashed back to its original position. With his feet sinking into the soft rich carpet, as though he were ankle-deep in some mossy bank, he stared about him at the great pictures which lined the walls.

"Surely, surely, I see Raphael's touch there," he cried, pointing up at the one which faced him.

"Yes, it is a Raphael, and I believe one of his best. I had a very exciting bid for it with the French Government. They wanted it for the Louvre, but of course at an auction the longest purse must win."

"And this 'Arrest of Catiline' must be a Rubens. One cannot mistake his splendid men and his infamous women."

"Yes, it is a Rubens. The other two are a Velasquez and a Teniers, fair specimens of the Spanish and of the Dutch schools. I have only old masters here. The moderns are in the billiard-room. The furniture here is a little curious. In fact, I fancy that it is unique. It is made of ebony and narwhals' horns. You see that the legs of everything are of spiral ivory, both the table and the chairs. It cost the upholsterer some little pains, for the supply of these things is a strictly limited one. Curiously enough, the Chinese Emperor had given a large order for narwhals' horns to repair some ancient pagoda, which was fenced in with them, but I outbid him in the market, and his celestial highness has had to wait. There is a lift here in the corner, but we do not need it. Pray step through this door. This is the billiard-room," he continued as they advanced into the adjoining room. "You see I have a few recent pictures of merit upon the walls. Here is a Corot, two Meissoniers, a Bouguereau, a Millais, an Orchardson, and two Alma-Tademas. It seems to me to be a pity to hang pictures over these walls of carved oak. Look at those birds hopping and singing in the branches. They really seem to move and twitter, don't they?"

"They are perfect. I never saw such exquisite work. But why do you call it a billiard-room, Mr. Haw? I do not see any board."

"Oh, a board is such a clumsy uncompromising piece of furniture. It is always in the way unless you actually need to use it. In this case the board is covered by that square of polished maple which you see let into the floor. You see!" As he spoke, the central portion of the flooring grew up, and a most beautiful tortoise-shell-plated billiard-table rose up to its proper position. He pressed a second spring, and a bagatelle-table appeared in the same fashion. "You may have card-tables or what you will by setting the levers in motion," he remarked. "But all this is very trifling. Perhaps we may find something in the museum which may be of more interest to you."

He led the way into another chamber, which was furnished in antique style, with hangings of the rarest and richest tapestry. The floor was a mosaic of coloured marbles, scattered over with mats of costly fur. There was little furniture, but a number of Louis Quatorze cabinets of ebony and silver with delicately-painted plaques were ranged round the apartment.

"It is perhaps hardly fair to dignify it by the name of a museum," said Raffles Haw. "It consists merely of a few elegant trifles which I have picked up here and there. Gems are my strongest point. I fancy that there, perhaps, I might challenge comparison with any private collector in the world. I lock them up, for even the best servants may be tempted."

He took a silver key from his watch chain, and began to unlock and draw out the drawers. A cry of wonder and of admiration burst from Robert McIntyre, as his eyes rested upon case after case filled with the most magnificent stones. The deep still red of the rubies, the clear scintillating green of the emeralds, the hard glitter of the diamonds, the many shifting shades of beryls, of amethysts, of onyxes, of cats'-eyes, of opals, of agates, of cornelians seemed to fill the whole chamber with a vague twinkling, many-coloured light. Long slabs of the beautiful blue lapis lazuli, magnificent bloodstones, specimens of pink and red and white coral, long strings of lustrous pearls, all these were tossed out by their owner as a careless schoolboy might pour marbles from his bag.

"This isn't bad," he said, holding up a great glowing yellow mass as large as his own head. "It is really a fine piece of amber. It was forwarded to me by my agent at the baltic. Twenty-eight pounds, it weighs. I never heard of so fine a one. I have no very large brilliants — there were no very large ones in the market — but my average is good. Pretty toys, are they not?" He picked up a double handful of emeralds from a drawer, and then let them trickle slowly back into the heap.

"Good heavens!" cried Robert, as he gazed from case to case. "It is an immense fortune in itself. Surely a hundred thousand pounds would hardly buy so splendid a collection."

"I don't think that you would do for a valuer of precious stones," said Raffles Haw, laughing. "Why, the contents of that one little drawer of brilliants could not be bought for the sum which you name. I have a memo. here of what I have expended up to date on my collection, though I have agents at work who will probably make very considerable additions to it within the next few weeks. As matters stand, however, I have spent — let me see — pearls one forty thousand; emeralds, seven fifty; rubies, eight forty; brilliants, nine twenty; onyxes — I have several very nice onyxes — two thirty. Other gems, carbuncles, agates — hum! Yes, it figures out at just over four million seven hundred and forty thousand. I dare say that we may say five millions, for I have not counted the odd money."

"Good gracious!" cried the young artist, with staring eyes.

"I have a certain feeling of duty in the matter. You see the cutting, polishing, and general sale of stones is one of the industries which is entirely dependent upon wealth. If we do not support it, it must languish, which means misfortune to a considerable number of people. The same applies to the gold filigree work which you noticed in the court. Wealth has its responsibilities, and the encouragement of these handicrafts are amongst the most obvious of them. Here is a nice ruby. It is Burmese, and the fifth largest in existence. I am inclined to think that if it were uncut it would be the second, but of course cutting takes away a great deal." He held up the blazing red stone, about the size of a chestnut, between his finger and thumb for a moment, and then threw it carelessly back into its drawer. "Come into the smoking-room," he said; "you will need some little refreshment, for they say that sight-seeing is the most exhausting occupation in the world."

In an instant a huge desert stretched on every side of them.

FROM CLIME TO CLIME

THE CHAMBER in which the bewildered Robert now found himself was more luxurious, if less rich, than any which he had yet seen. Low settees of claret-coloured plush were scattered in orderly disorder over a mossy Eastern carpet. Deep lounges, reclining sofas, American rocking-chairs, all were to be had for the choosing. One end of the room was walled by glass, and appeared to open upon a luxuriant hot-house. At the further end a double line of gilt rails supported a profusion of the most recent magazines and periodicals. A rack at each side of the inlaid fireplace sustained a long line of the pipes of all places and nations — English cherrywoods, French briars, German china-bowls, carved meerschaums, scented cedar and myallwood, with Eastern narghiles, Turkish chibooques, and two great golden-topped hookahs. To right and left were a series of small lockers, extending in a treble row for the whole length of the room, with the names of the various brands of tobacco scrolled in ivory work across them. Above were other larger tiers of polished oak, which held cigars and cigarettes.

"Try that Damascus settee," said the master of the house, as he threw himself into a rocking-chair. "It is from the Sultan's upholsterer. The Turks have a very good notion of comfort. I am a confirmed smoker myself, Mr. McIntyre, so I have been able, perhaps, to check my architect here more than in most of the other departments. Of pictures, for example, I know nothing, as you would very speedily find out. On a tobacco, I might, perhaps, offer an opinion. Now these"—he drew out some long, beautifully-rolled, mellow-coloured cigars—"these are really something a little out of the common. Do try one."

Robert lit and weed which was offered to him, and leaned back luxuriously amid his cushions, gazing through the blue balmy fragrant cloud-wreaths at the extraordinary man in the dirty pea-jacket who spoke of millions as another might of sovereigns. With his pale face, his sad, languid air, and his bowed shoulders, it was as though he were crushed down under the weight of his own gold. There was a mute apology, an attitude of deprecation in his manner and speech, which was strangely at variance with the immense power which he wielded. To Robert the whole whimsical incident had been intensely interesting and amusing. His artistic nature blossomed out in this atmosphere of perfect luxury and comfort, and he was conscious of a sense of repose and of absolute sensual contentment such as he had never before experienced.

"Shall it be coffee, or Rhine wine, or Tokay, or perhaps something stronger?" asked Raffles Haw, stretching out his hand to what looked like a piano-board projecting from the wall. "I can recommend the Tokay. I have it from the man who supplies the Emperor of Austria, though I think I may say that I get the cream of it."

He struck twice upon one of the piano-notes, and sat

expectant. With a sharp click at the end of ten seconds a sliding shutter flew open, and a small tray protruded bearing two long tapering Venetian glasses filled with wine.

"It works very nicely," said Raffles Haw. "It is quite a new thing — never before done, as far as I know. You see the names of the various wines and so on printed on the notes. By pressing the note down I complete an electric circuit which causes the tap in the cellars beneath to remain open long enough to fill the glass which always stands beneath it. The glasses, you understand, stand upon a revolving drum, so that there must always be one there. The glasses are then brought up through a pneumatic tube, which is set working by the increased weight of the glass when the wine is added to it. It is a pretty little idea. But I am afraid that I bore you rather with all these petty contrivances. It is a whim of mine to push mechanism as far as it will go."

"On the contrary, I am filled with interest and wonder," said Robert warmly. "It is as if I had been suddenly whipped up out of prosaic old England and transferred in an instant to some enchanted palace, some Eastern home of the Genii. I could not have believed that there existed upon this earth such adaptation of means to an end, such complete mastery of every detail which may aid in stripping life of any of its petty worries."

"I have something yet to show you," remarked Raffles Haw; "but we will rest here for a few minutes, for I wished to have a word with you. How is the cigar?"

"Most excellent."

"It was rolled in Louisiana in the old slavery days. There is nothing made like them now. The man who had them did not know their value. He let them go at merely a few shillings apiece. Now I want you to do me a favour, Mr. McIntyre."

"I shall be so glad."

"You can see more or less how I am situated. I am a complete stranger here. With the well-to-do classes I have little in common. I am no society man. I don't want to call or be called on. I am a student in a small way, and a man of quiet tastes. I have no social ambitions at all. Do you understand?"

"Entirely."

"On the other hand, my experience of the world has been that it is the rarest of things to be able to form a friendship with a poorer man — I mean with a man who is at all eager to increase his income. They think much of your wealth, and little of yourself. I have tried, you understand, and I know." He paused and ran his fingers through his thin beard.

Robert McIntyre nodded to show that he appreciated his position.

"Now, you see," he continued, "if I am to be cut off from the rich by my own tastes, and from those who are not rich by my distrust of their motives, my situation is an isolated one. Not that I mind isolation: I am used to it. But it limits my field of usefulness. I have no trustworthy means of informing myself when and where I may do good. I have already, I am glad to say, met a man to-day, your vicar, who appears to be thoroughly unselfish and trustworthy. He shall be one of my channels of communication with the outer world. Might I ask you whether you would be willing to become another?"

"With the greatest pleasure," said Robert eagerly.

The proposition filled his heart with joy, for it

seemed to give him an almost official connection with this paradise of a house. He could not have asked for anything more to his taste.

"I was fortunate enough to discover by your conversation how high a ground you take in such matters, and how entirely disinterested you are. You may have observed that I was short and almost rude with you at first. I have had reason to fear and suspect all chance friendships. Too often they have proved to be carefully planned beforehand, with some sordid object in view. Good heavens, what stories I could tell you! A lady pursued by a bull — I have risked my life to save her, and have learned afterwards that the scene had been arranged by the mother as an effective introduction, and that the bull had been hired by the hour. But I won't shake your faith in human nature. I have had some rude shocks myself. I look, perhaps, with a jaundiced eye on all who come near me. It is the more needful that I should have one whom I can trust to advise me."

"If you will only show me where my opinion can be of any use I shall be most happy," said Robert. "My people come from Birmingham, but I know most of the folk here and their position."

"That is just what I want. Money can do so much good, and it may do so much harm. I shall consult you when I am in doubt. By the way, there is one small question which I might ask you now. Can you tell me who a young lady is with very dark hair, grey eyes, and a finely chiselled face? She wore a blue dress when I saw her, with astrachan about her neck and cuffs."

Robert chuckled to himself.

"I know that dress pretty well," he said. "It is my sister Laura whom you describe."

"Your sister! Really! Why, there is a resemblance, now that my attention is called to it. I saw her the other day, and wondered who she might be. She lives with you, of course?"

"Yes; my father, she, and I live together at Elmdene."

"Where I hope to have the pleasure of making their acquaintance. You have finished your cigar? Have another, or try a pipe. To the real smoker all is mere trifling save the pipe. I have most brands of tobacco here. The lockers are filled on the Monday, and on Saturday they are handed over to the old folk at the almshouses, so I manage to keep it pretty fresh always. Well, if you won't take anything else, perhaps you would care to see one or two of the other effects which I have devised. On this side is the armoury, and beyond it the library. My collection of books is a limited one; there are just over the fifty thousand volumes. But it is to some extent remarkable for quality. I have a Visigoth Bible of the fifth century, which I rather fancy is unique; there is a *Biblia Pauperum* of 1430; a MS. of Genesis done upon mulberry leaves, probably of the second century; a *Tristan and Iseult* of the eighth century; and some hundred black-letters, with five very fine specimens of Schoffer and Fust. But those you may turn over any wet afternoon when you have nothing better to do. Meanwhile, I have a little device connected with this smoking-room which may amuse you. Light this other cigar. Now sit with me upon this lounge which stands at the further end of the room."

The sofa in question was in a niche which was lined in three sides and above with perfectly clear transparent crystal. As they sat down the master of the house drew a cord which pulled out a crystal shutter behind them, so that they were enclosed on all sides in a great box of glass, so pure and so highly polished that its presence might very easily be forgotten. A number of golden cords with crystal handles hung down into this small chamber, and appeared to be connected with a long shining bar outside.

"Now, where would you like to smoke your cigar?" said Raffles Haw, with a twinkle in his demure eyes. "Shall we go to India, or to Egypt, or to China, or to——"

"To South America," said Robert.

There was a twinkle, a whirr, and a sense of motion. The young artist gazed about him in absolute amazement. Look where he would all round were tree-ferns and palms with long drooping creepers, and a blaze of brilliant orchids. Smoking-room, house, England, all were gone, and he sat on a settee in the heart of a virgin forest of the Amazon. It was no mere optical delusion or trick. He could see the hot steam rising from the tropical undergrowth, the heavy drops falling from the huge green leaves, the very grain and fibre of the rough bark which clothed the trunks. Even as he gazed a green mottled snake curled noiselessly over a branch above his head, and a bright-coloured paroquet broke suddenly from amid the foliage and flashed off among the tree-trunks. Robert gazed around, speechless with surprise, and finally turned upon his host a face in which curiosity was not unmixed with a suspicion of fear.

"People have been burned for less, have they not?" cried Raffles Haw, laughing heartily. "Have you had enough of the Amazon? What do you say to a spell of Egypt?"

Again the whirr, the swift flash of passing objects, and in an instant a huge desert stretched on every side of them, as far as the eye could reach. In the foreground a clump of five palm-trees towered into the air, with a profusion of rough cactus-like plants bristling from their base. On the other side rose a rugged, gnarled, grey monolith, carved at the base into a huge scarabaeus. A group of lizards played about on the surface of the old carved stone. Beyond, the yellow sand stretched away into furthest space, where the dim mirage mist played along the horizon.

"Mr. Haw, I cannot understand it!"

Robert grasped the velvet edge of the settee, and gazed wildly about him.

"The effect is rather startling, is it not? This Egyptian desert is my favourite when I lay myself out for a contemplative smoke. It seems strange that tobacco should have come from the busy, practical West. It has much more affinity for the dreamy, languid East. But perhaps you would like to run over to China for a change?"

"Not to-day," said Robert, passing his hand over his forehead. "I feel rather confused by all these wonders, and indeed I think that they have affected my nerves a little. Besides, it is time that I returned to my prosaic Elmdene, if I can find my way out of this wilderness to which you have transplanted me. But would you ease my mind, Mr. Haw, by showing me how this thing is done?"

"It is the merest toy—a complex plaything, nothing more. Allow me to explain. I have a line of very large green-houses which extends from one end of my smoking-room. These different houses are kept at varying degrees of heat and humidity so as to reproduce the exact climates of Egypt, China, and the rest. You see, our crystal chamber is a tramway running with a minimum of friction along a steel rod. By pulling this or that handle I regulate how far it shall go, and it travels, as you have seen, with amazing speed. The effect of my hot-houses is heightened by the roofs being invariably concealed by skies, which are really very admirably painted, and by the introduction of birds and other creatures, which seem to flourish quite as well in artificial as in natural heat. This explains the South American effect."

"But not the Egyptian."

"No. It is certainly rather clever. I had the best man in France, at least the best at those large effects, to paint in that circular background. You understand, the palms, cacti, obelisk, and so on, are perfectly genuine, and so is the sand for fifty yards or so, and I defy the keenest-eyed man in England to tell where the deception commences. It is the familiar and perhaps rather meretricious effect of a circular panorama, but carried out in the most complete manner. Was there any other point?"

"The crystal box? Why was it?"

"To preserve my guests from the effects of the changes of temperature. It would be a poor kindness to bring them back to my smoking-room drenched through, and with the seeds of a violent cold. The crystal has to be kept warm, too, otherwise vapour would deposit, and you would have your view spoiled. But must you really go? Then here we are back in the smoking-room. I hope that it will not be your last visit by many a one. And if I may come down to Elmdene I should be very glad to do so. This is the way through the museum."

As Robert McIntyre emerged from the balmy aromatic atmosphere of the great house, into the harsh, raw, biting air of an English winter evening, he felt as though he had been away for a long visit in some foreign country. Time is measured by impressions, and so vivid and novel had been his feelings, that weeks and weeks might have elapsed since his chat with the smoke-grimed stranger in the road. He walked along with his head in a whirl, his whole mind possessed and intoxicated by the one idea of the boundless wealth and the immense power of this extraordinary stranger. Small and sordid and mean seemed his own Elmdene as he approached it, and he passed over its threshold full of restless discontent against himself and his surroundings.

V

Laura's Request

THAT NIGHT after supper Robert McIntyre poured forth all that he had seen to his father and to his sister. So full was he of the one subject that it was a relief to him to share his knowledge with others. Rather for his own sake, then, than for theirs he depicted vividly all the marvels which he had seen; the profusion of wealth, the regal treasure-house of gems, the gold, the marble, the extraordinary devices, the absolute lavishness and complete disregard for money which was shown in every detail. For an hour he pictured with glowing words all the wonders which had been shown him, and ended with some pride by describing the request which Mr. Raffles Haw had made, and the complete confidence which he had placed in him.

His words had a very different effect upon his two listeners. Old McIntyre leaned back in his chair with a bitter smile upon his lips, his thin face crinkled into a thousand puckers, and his small eyes shining with envy and greed. His lean yellow hand upon the table was clenched until the knuckles gleamed white in the lamplight. Laura, on the other hand, leaned forward, her lips parted, drinking in her brother's words with a glow of colour upon either cheek. It seemed to Robert, as he glanced from one to the other of them, that he had never seen his father look so evil, or his sister so beautiful.

"Who is the fellow, then?" asked the old man after a considerable pause. "I hope he got all this in an honest fashion. Five millions in jewels, you say. Good gracious me! Ready to give it away, too, but afraid of pauperizing any one. You can tell him, Robert, that you know of one very deserving case which has not the slightest objection to being pauperized."

"But who can he possibly be, Robert?" cried Laura. "Haw cannot be his real name. He must be some disguised prince, or perhaps a king in exile. Oh, I should have loved to have seen those diamonds and the emeralds! I always think that emeralds suit dark people best. You must tell me again all about that museum, Robert."

"I don't think that he is anything more than he pretends to be," her brother answered. "He has the plain, quiet manners of an ordinary middle-class Englishman. There was no particular polish that I could see. He knew a little about books and pictures, just enough to appreciate them, but nothing more. No, I fancy that he is a man quite in our own position of life, who has in some way inherited a vast sum. Of course it is difficult for me to form an estimate, but I should judge that what I saw to-day — house, pictures, jewels, books, and so on — could never have been bought under twenty millions, and I am sure that figure is entirely an under-statement."

"I never knew but one Haw," said old McIntyre, drumming his fingers on the table; "he was a foreman in my pin-fire cartridge-case department. But he was

an elderly single man. Well, I hope he got it all honestly.
I hope the money is clean."

"And really, really, he is coming to see us!" cried
Laura, clapping her hands. "Oh, when do you think he
will come, Robert? Do give me warning. Do you think
it will be to-morrow?"

"I am sure I cannot say."

"I should so love to see him. I don't know when I
have been so interested."

"Why, you have a letter there," remarked Robert.
"From Hector, too, by the foreign stamp. How is he?"

"It only came this evening. I have not opened it yet.
To tell the truth, I have been so interested in your story
that I had forgotten all about it. Poor old Hector! It is
from Madeira." She glanced rapidly over the four
pages of straggling writing in the young sailor's bold
schoolboyish hand. "Oh, he is all right," she said.
"They had a gale on the way out, and that sort of thing.
but he is all right now. He thinks he may be back by
March. I wonder whether your new friend will come
to-morrow — your knight of the enchanted Castle."

"Hardly so soon, I should fancy."

"If he should be looking about for an investment,
Robert," said the father, "you won't forget to tell him
what a fine opening there is now in the gun trade. With
my knowledge, and a few thousands at my back, I
could bring him in his thirty per cent. as regular as the
bank. After all, he must lay out his money somehow.
He cannot sink it all in books and precious stones. I am
sure that I could give him the highest references."

"It may be a long time before he comes, father," said
Robert coldly; "and when he does I am afraid that I
can hardly use his friendship as a means of advancing
your interest."

"We are his equals, father," cried Laura with spirit. "Would you put us on the footing of beggars? He would think we cared for him only for his money. I wonder that you should think of such a thing."

"If I had not thought of such things where would your education have been, miss?" retorted the angry old man; and Robert stole quietly away to his room, whence amid his canvases he could still hear the hoarse voice and the clear in their never-ending family jangle. More and more sordid seemed the surroundings of his life, and more and more to be valued the peace which money can buy.

Breakfast had hardly been cleared in the morning, and Robert had not yet ascended to his work, when there came a timid tapping at the door, and there was Raffles Haw on the mat outside. Robert ran out and welcomed him with all cordiality.

"I am afraid that I am a very early visitor," he said apologetically; "but I often take a walk after breakfast." He had no traces of work upon him now, but was trim and neat with a dark suit, and carefully brushed hair. "You spoke yesterday of your work. Perhaps, early as it is, you would allow me the privilege of looking over your studio?"

"Pray step in, Mr. Haw," cried Robert, all in a flutter at this advance from so munificent a patron of art; "I should be only too happy to show you such little work as I have on hand, though, indeed, I am almost afraid when I think how familiar you are with some of the greatest masterpieces. Allow me to introduce you to my father and to my sister Laura."

Old McIntyre bowed low and rubbed his thin hands together; but the young lady gave a gasp of surprise, and stared with widely-opened eyes at the millionaire.

Haw stepped forward, however, and shook her quietly by the hand.

"I expected to find that it was you," he said. "I have already met your sister, Mr. McIntyre, on the very first day that I came here. We took shelter in a shed from a snowstorm, and had quite a pleasant little chat."

"I had no notion that I was speaking to the owner of the Hall," said Laura in some confusion. "How funnily things turn out, to be sure!"

"I had often wondered who it was that I spoke to, but it was only yesterday that I discovered. What a sweet little place you have here! It must be charming in summer. Why, if it were not for this hill my windows would look straight across at yours."

"Yes, and we should see all your beautiful plantations," said Laura, standing beside him in the window. "I was wishing only yesterday that the hill was not there."

"Really! I shall be happy to have it removed for you if you would like it."

"Good gracious!" cried Laura. "Why, where would you put it?"

"Oh, they could run it along the line and dump it anywhere. It is not much of a hill. A few thousand men with proper machinery, and a line of rails brought right up to them could easily dispose of it in a few months."

"And the poor vicar's house?" Laura asked, laughing.

"I think that might be got over. We could run him up a fac-simile, which would, perhaps, be more convenient to him. Your brother will tell you that I am quite an expert at the designing of houses. But, seriously, if you think it would be an improvement I will see what can be done."

"Not for the world, Mr. Haw. Why, I should be a

traitor to the whole village if I were to encourage such a scheme. The hill is the one thing which gives Tamfield the slightest individuality. It would be the height of selflishness to sacrifice it in order to improve the view from Elmdene."

"It is a little box of a place this, Mr. Haw," said old McIntyre. "I should think you must feel quite stifled in it after your grand mansion, of which my sons tells me such wonders. But we were not always accustomed to this sort of thing, Mr. Haw. Humble as I stand here, there was a time, and not so long ago, when I could write as many figures on a cheque as any gunmaker in Birmingham. It was ——"

"He is a dear discontented old papa," cried Laura, throwing her arm round him in a caressing manner. He gave a sharp squeak and a grimace of pain, which he endeavoured to hide by an outbreak of painfully artificial coughing.

"Shall we go upstairs?" said Robert hurriedly, anxious to divert his guest's attention from this little domestic incident. "My studio is the real atelier, for it is right up under the tiles. I shall lead the way, if you will have the kindness to follow me."

Leaving Laura and Mr. McIntyre, they went up together to the workroom. Mr. Haw stood long in front of the "Signing of Magna Charta," and the "Murder of Thomas à Becket," screwing up his eyes and twitching nervously at his beard, while Robert stood by in anxious expectancy.

"And how much are these?" asked Raffles Haw at last.

"I priced them at a hundred apiece when I sent them to London."

"Then the best I can wish you is that the day may

come when you would gladly give ten times the sum to have them back again. I am sure that there are great possibilities in you, and I see that in grouping and in boldness of design you have already achieved much. But your drawing, if you will excuse my saying so, is just a little crude, and your colouring perhaps a trifle thin. Now, I will make a bargain with you, Mr. McIntyre, if you will consent to it. I know that money has no charms for you, but still, as you said when I first met you, a man must live. I shall buy these two canvases from you at the price which you name, subject to the condition that you may always have them back again by repaying the same sum."

"You are really very kind." Robert hardly knew whether to be delighted at having sold his pictures or humiliated at the frank criticism of the buyer.

"May I write a cheque at once?" said Raffles Haw. "Here is pen and ink. So! I shall send a couple of footmen down for them in the afternoon. Well, I shall keep them in trust for you. I dare say that when you are famous they will be of value as specimens of your early manner."

"I am sure that I am extremely obliged to you, Mr. Haw," said the young artist, placing the cheque in his notebook. He glanced at it as he folded it up, in the vague hope that perhaps this man of whims had assessed his pictures at a higher rate than he had named. The figures, however, were exact. Robert began dimly to perceive that there were drawbacks as well as advantages to the reputation of a money-scorner, which he had gained by a few chance words, prompted rather by the reaction against his father's than by his own real convictions.

"I hope, Miss McIntyre," said Raffles Haw, when

they had descended to the sitting-room once more, "that you will do me the honour of coming to see the little curiosities which I have gathered together. Your brother will, I am sure, escort you up; or perhaps Mr. McIntyre would care to come?"

"I shall be delighted to come, Mr. Haw," cried Laura, with her sweetest smile. "A good deal of my time just now is taken up in looking after the poor people, who find the cold weather very trying." Robert raised his eyebrows, for it was the first he had heard of his sister's missions of mercy, but Mr. Raffles Haw nodded approvingly. "Robert was telling us of your wonderful hot-houses. I am sure I wish I could transport the whole parish into one of them, and give them a good warm."

"Nothing would be easier, but I am afraid that they might find it a little trying when they come out again. I have one house which is only just finished. Your brother has not seen it yet, but I think it is the best of them all. It represents an Indian jungle, and is hot enough in all conscience."

"I shall so look forward to seeing it," cried Laura, clasping her hands. "It has been one of the dreams of my life to see India. I have read so much of it, the temples, the forests, the great rivers, and the tigers. Why, you would hardly believe it, but I have never seen a tiger except in a picture."

"That can easily be set right," said Raffles Haw, with his quiet smile. "Would you care to see one?"

"Oh, immensely."

"I will have one sent down. Let me see, it is nearly twelve o'clock. I can get a wire to Liverpool by one. There is a man there who deals in such things. I should think he would be due to-morrow morning. Well, I

shall look forward to seeing you all before very long. I
have rather outstayed my time, for I am a man of
routine, and I always put in a certain number of hours
in my laboratory." He shook hands cordially with them
all, and lighting his pipe at the doorstep, strolled off
upon his way.

"Well, what do you think of him now?" asked
Robert, as they watched his black figure against the
white snow.

"I think that he is no more fit to be trusted with all
that money than a child," cried the old man. "It made
me positively sick to hear him talk of moving hills and
buying tigers, and such-like nonsense, when there are
honest men without a business, and great businesses
starving for a little capital. It's unchristian — that's what
I call it."

"I think he is most delightful, Robert," said Laura.
"Remember, you have promised to take us up to the
Hall. And he evidently wishes us to go soon. Don't you
think we might go this afternoon?"

"I hardly think that, Laura. You leave it in my
hands, and I will arrange it all. And now I must get to
work, for the light is so very short on these winter
days."

That night Robert McIntire had gone to bed, and
was dozing off when a hand plucked at his shoulder,
and he started up to find his sister in some white
drapery, with a shawl thrown over her shoulders,
standing beside him in the moonlight.

"Robert, dear," she whispered, stooping over him,
"there was something I wanted to ask you, but papa
was always in the way. You will do something to please
me, won't you, Robert?"

"Of course, Laura. What is it?"

"I do so hate having my affairs talked over, dear. If Mr. Raffles Haw says anything to you about me, or asks any questions, please don't say anything about Hector. You won't, will you, Robert, for the sake of your little sister?"

"No; not unless you wish it."

"There is a dear good brother."

She stooped over him and kissed him tenderly.

It was a rare thing for Laura to show any emotion, and her brother marvelled sleepily over it until he relapsed into his interrupted doze.

A Strange Visitor

THE McIntyre family was seated at breakfast on the morning which followed the first visit of Raffles Haw, when they were surprised to hear the buzz and hum of a multitude of voices in the village street. Nearer and nearer came the tumult, and then, of a sudden, two maddened horses reared themselves up on the other side of the garden hedge, prancing and pawing, with ears laid back and eyes ever glancing at some horror behind them. Two men hung shouting to their bridles, while a third came rushing up the curved gravel path. Before the McIntyres could realize the situation, their maid, Mary, darted into the sitting-room with terror in her round freckled face:

"If you please, miss," she screamed, "your tiger has arrove."

"Good heavens!" cried Robert, rushing to the door with his half-filled teacup in his hand. "This is too much. Here is an iron cage on a trolly with a great ramping tiger, and the whole village with their mouths open."

"Mad as a hatter!" shrieked old Mr. McIntyre. "I could see it in his eye. He spent enough on this beast to start me in business. Whoever heard of such a thing? Tell the driver to take it to the police-station."

"Nothing of the sort, papa," said Laura, rising with dignity and wrapping a shawl about her shoulders. Her eyes were shining, her cheeks flushed, and she carried herself like a triumphant queen.

Robert, with his teacup in his hand, allowed his attention to be diverted from their strange visitor while he gazed at his beautiful sister.

"Mr. Raffles Haw has done this out of kindness to me," she said, sweeping towards the door. "I look upon it as a great attention on his part. I shall certainly go out and look at it."

"If you please, sir," said the carman, reappearing at the door, "it's all as we can do to 'old in the 'osses."

"Let us all go out together then," suggested Robert.

They went as far as the garden fence and stared over, while the whole village, from the school-children to the old grey-haired men from the almshouses, gathered round in mute astonishment. The tiger, a long, lithe, venomous-looking creature, with two blazing green eyes, paced stealthily round the little cage, lashing its sides with its tail, and rubbing its muzzle against the bars.

"What were your orders?" asked Robert of the carman.

"It came through by special express from Liverpool, sir, and the train is drawn up at the Tamfield siding all ready to take it back. If it 'ad been royalty the railway folk couldn't ha' shown it more respec'. We are to take it back when you're done with it. It's been a cruel job, sir, for our arms is pulled clean out of the sockets a-'olding in of the 'osses."

"What a dear, sweet creature it is," cried Laura. "How sleek and how graceful! I cannot understand how people could be afraid of anything so beautiful."

"If you please, marm," said the carman, touching his skin cap, "he out with his paw between the bars as we stood in the station yard, and if I 'adn't pulled my mate Bill back it would ha' been a case of kingdom come. It was a proper squeak, I can tell ye."

"I never saw anything more lovely," continued Laura, loftily overlooking the remarks of the driver. "It has been a very great pleasure to me to see it, and I hope that you will tell Mr. Haw so if you see him, Robert."

"The horses are very restive," said her brother. "Perhaps, Laura, if you have seen enough, it would be as well to let them go."

She bowed in the regal fashion which she had so suddenly adopted. Robert shouted the order, the driver sprang up, his comrades let the horses go, and away rattled the waggon and the trolly with half the Tamfielders streaming vainly behind it.

"Is it not wonderful what money can do?" Laura remarked, as they knocked the snow from their shoes within the porch. "There seems to be no wish which Mr. Haw could not at once gratify."

"No wish of yours, you mean," broke in her father. "It's different when he is dealing with a wrinkled old man who has spent himself in working for his children. A plainer case of love at first sight I never saw."

"How can you be so coarse, papa?" cried Laura, but her eyes flashed, and her teeth gleamed, as though the remark had not altogether displeased her.

"For heaven's sake, be careful, Laura!" cried Robert. "It had not struck me before, but really it does look rather like it. You know how you stand. Raffles Haw is not a man to play with."

"You dear old boy!" said Laura, laying her hand

upon his shoulder, "what do you know of such things? All you have to do is to go on with your painting, and to remember the promise you made the other night."

"What promise was that, then?" cried old McIntyre suspiciously.

"Never you mind, papa. But if you forget it, Robert, I shall never forgive you as long as I live."

VII

THE WORKINGS OF WEALTH

I T can easily be believed that as the weeks passed the name and fame of the mysterious owner of the New Hall resounded over the quiet country side until the rumour of him had spread to the remotest corners of Warwickshire and Staffordshire. In Birmingham on the one side, and in Coventry and Leamington on the other, there was gossip as to his untold riches, his extraordinary whims, and the remarkable life which he led. His name was bandied from mouth to mouth, and a thousand efforts were made to find out who and what he was. In spite of all their plans, however, the newsmongers were unable to discover the slightest trace of his antecedents, or to form even a guess as to the secret of his riches.

It was no wonder that conjecture was rife upon the subject, for hardly a day passed without furnishing some new instance of the boundlessness of his power and of the goodness of his heart. Through the vicar, Robert, and others, he had learned much of the inner life of the parish, and many were the times when the struggling man, harassed and driven to the wall, found thrust into his hand some morning a brief note with an enclosure which rolled all the sorrow back from his life. One day a thick double-breasted pea-jacket and a pair of good sturdy boots were served out to every man in the almshouse. On another, Miss Swire, the decayed gentlewoman who eked out her small annuity by needlework, had a brand new first-class sewing-machine handed in to her to take the place of the old worn-out treadle which tried her rheumatic joints. The pale-faced schoolmaster, who had spent years with hardly a break in struggling with the juvenile obtuseness of Tamfield, received through the post a circular ticket for a two months' tour through Southern Europe, with hotel coupons and all complete. John Hackett, the farmer, after five long years of bad seasons, borne with a brave heart, had at last been overthrown by the sixth, and had the bailiffs actually in the house when the good vicar had rushed in, waving a note above his head, to tell him not only that his deficit had been made up, but that enough remained over to provide the improved machinery which would enable him to hold his own for the future. An almost superstitious feeling came upon the rustic folk as they looked at the great palace when the sun gleamed upon the huge hot-houses, or even more so, perhaps, when at night the brilliant electric lights shot their white radiance through the countless rows of windows. To them it was as if some minor Providence presided in that great place, unseen but seeing all, boundless in its power and its graciousness, ever ready to assist and to befriend. In every good deed, however, Raffles Haw still remained in the background, while the vicar and Robert had the pleasant task of conveying his benefits to the lowly and the suffering.

Once only did he appear in his own person, and that was upon the famous occasion when he saved the well-known bank of Garraweg Brothers in Birmingham.

The most charitable and upright of men, the two brothers, Louis and Rupert, had built up a business which extended its ramifications into every townlet of four counties. The failure of their London agents had suddenly brought a heavy loss upon them, and the circumstance leaking out had caused a sudden and most dangerous run upon their establishment. Urgent telegrams for bullion from all their forty branches poured in at the very instant when the head office was crowded with anxious clients all waving their deposit-books, and clamouring for their money. Bravely did the two brothers with their staff stand with smiling faces behind the shining counter, while swift messengers sped and telegrams flashed to draw in all the available resources of the bank. All day the stream poured through the office, and when four o'clock came, and the doors were closed for the day, the street without was still blocked by the expectant crowd, while there remained scarce a thousand pounds of bullion in the cellars.

"It is only postponed, Louis," said brother Rupert despairingly, when the last clerk had left the office, and when at last they could relax the fixed smile upon their haggard faces.

"Those shutters will never come down again," cried brother Louis, and the two suddenly burst out sobbing in each other's arms, not for their own griefs, but for the miseries which they might bring upon those who had trusted them.

But who shall ever dare to say that there is no hope, if he will but give his griefs to the world? That very night Mrs. Spurling had received a letter from her old school friend, Mrs. Louis Garraweg, with all her fears and her hopes poured out in it, and the whole sad story of their troubles. Swift from the Vicarage went the message to the Hall, and early next morning Mr. Raffles Haw, with a great black carpet-bag in his hand, found means to draw the cashier of the local branch of the Bank of England from his breakfast, and to persuade him to open his doors at unofficial hours. By half-past nine the crowd had already begun to collect around Garraweg's, when a stranger, pale and thin, with a bloated carpet-bag, was shown at his own very pressing request into the bank parlour.

"It is no use, sir," said the elder brother humbly, as they stood together encouraging each other to turn a brave face to misfortune, "we can do no more. We have little left, and it would be unfair to the others to pay you now. We can but hope that when our assets are realized no one will be the loser save ourselves."

"I did not come to draw out, but to put in," said Raffles Haw in his demure apologetic fashion. "I have in my bag five thousand hundred-pound Bank of England notes. If you will have the goodness to place them to my credit account I should be extremely obliged."

"But, good heavens, sir!" stammered Rupert Garraweg, "have you not heard? Have you not seen? We cannot allow you to do this thing blindfold; can we, Louis?"

"Most certainly not. We cannot recommend our bank, sir, at the present moment, for there is a run upon us, and we do not know to what lengths it may go."

"Tut! tut!" said Raffles Haw. "If the run continues you must send me a wire, and I shall make a small addition to my account. You will send me a receipt by post. Good-morning, gentlemen!" He bowed himself out ere the astounded partners could realize what had befallen them, or raise their eyes from the huge black bag and the visiting card which lay upon their table. There was no great failure in Birmingham that day, and the house of Garraweg still survives to enjoy the success which it deserves.

Such were the deeds by which Raffles Haw made himself known throughout the Midlands, and yet, in spite of all his open-handedness, he was not a man to be imposed upon. In vain the sturdy beggar cringed at his gate, and in vain the crafty letter-writer poured out a thousand fabulous woes upon paper. Robert was astonished when he brought some tale of trouble to the Hall to observe how swift was the perception of the recluse, and how unerringly he could detect a flaw in a narrative, or lay his finger upon the one point which rang false. Were a man strong enough to help himself, or of such a nature as to profit nothing by help, none would he get from the master of the New Hall. In vain, for example, did old McIntyre throw himself continually across the path of the millionaire, and impress upon him, by a thousand hints and innuendoes, the hard fortune which had been dealt him, and the ease with which his fallen greatness might be restored. Raffles Haw listened politely, bowed, smiled, but never showed the slightest inclination to restore the querulous old gunmaker to his pedestal.

But if the recluse's wealth was a lure which drew the beggars from far and near, as the lamp draws the moths, it had the same power of attraction upon another and much more dangerous class. Strange hard faces were seen in the village street, prowling figures were marked at night stealing about among the fir plantations, and warning messages arrived from city police and county constabulary to say that evil visitors were known to have taken train to Tamfield. But if, as Raffles Haw held, there were few limits to the power of immense wealth, it possessed, among other things, the power of self-preservation, as one or two people were to learn to their cost.

"Would you mind stepping up to the Hall?" he said one morning, putting his head in at the door of the Elmdene sitting-room. "I have something there that might amuse you." He was on intimate terms with the McIntyres now, and there were few days on which they did not see something of each other.

They gladly accompanied him, all three, for such invitations were usually the prelude of some agreeable surprise which he had in store for them.

"I have shown you a tiger," he remarked to Laura, as he led them into the dining-room. "I will now show you something quite as dangerous, though not nearly so pretty." There was an arrangement of mirrors at one end of the room, with a large circular glass set at a sharp angle at the top.

"Look in there—in the upper glass," said Raffles Haw.

"Good gracious! what dreadful-looking men!" cried Laura. "There are two of them, and I don't know which is the worse."

"What on earth are they doing?" asked Robert. "They appear to be sitting on the ground in some sort of a cellar."

"Most dangerous-looking characters," said the old man. "I should strongly recommend you to send for a policeman."

"I have done so. But it seems a work of supereroga-tion to take them to prison, for they are very snugly in prison already. However, I suppose that the law must have its own."

"And who are they, and how did they come there? Do tell us, Mr. Haw."

Laura McIntyre had a pretty beseeching way with her, which went rather piquantly with her queenly style of beauty.

"I know no more than you do. They were not there last night, and they are here this morning, so I suppose it is a safe inference that they came in during the night, especially as my servants found the window open when they came down. As to their character and intentions, I should think that is pretty legible upon their faces. They look a pair of beauties, don't they?"

"But I cannot understand in the least where they are," said Robert, staring into the mirror. "One of them has taken to butting his head against the wall. No, he is bending so that the other may stand upon his back. He is up there now, and the light is shining upon his face. What a bewildered ruffianly face it is too. I should so like to sketch it. It would be a study for the picture I am thinking of the Reign of Terror."

"I have caught them in my patent burglar trap," said Haw. "They are my first birds, but I have no doubt that they will not be the last. I will show you how it works. It is quite a new thing. This flooring is now as strong as possible, but every night I disconnect it. It is done simultaneously by a central machine for every room on the ground-floor. When the floor is disconnected one may advance three or four steps, either from the window or door, and then that whole part turns on a hinge and slides you into a padded strong-room beneath, where you may kick your heels until you are released. There is a central oasis between the hinges, where the furniture is grouped for the night. The flooring flies into position again when the weight of the intruder is removed, and there he must bide, while I can always take a peep at him by this simple little optical arrangement. I thought it might amuse you to have a look at my prisoners before I handed them over to the head-constable, who I see is now coming up the avenue."

"The poor burglars!" cried Laura. "It is no wonder that they look bewildered, for I suppose, Mr. Haw, that they neither know where they are, nor how they came there. I am so glad to know that you guard yourself in this way, for I have often thought that you ran a danger."

"Have you so?" said he, smiling round at her. "I think that my house is fairly burglar-proof. I have one window which may be used as an entrance, the centre one of the three of my laboratory. I keep it so because, to tell the truth, I am somewhat of a night prowler myself, and when I treat myself to a ramble under the stars I like to slip in and out without ceremony. It would, however, be a fortunate rogue who picked the only safe entrance out of a hundred, and even then he might find pitfalls. Here is the constable, but you must not go, for Miss McIntyre has still something to see in my little place. If you will step into the billiard-room I shall be with you in a very few moments."

VIII

A BILLIONAIRE'S PLANS

THAT MORNING, and many mornings both before and afterwards, were spent by Laura at the New Hall examining the treasures of the museum, playing with the thousand costly toys which Raffles Haw had collected, or sallying out from the smoking-room in the cyrstal chamber into the long line of luxurious hot-houses. Haw would walk demurely beside her as she flitted from one thing to another like a butterfly among flowers, watching her out of the corner of his eyes, and taking a quiet pleasure in her delight. The only joy which his costly possessions had ever brought him was that which came from the entertainment of others.

By this time his attentions towards Laura McIntyre had become so marked that they could hardly be mistaken. He visibly brightened in her presence, and was never weary of devising a thousand methods of surprising and pleasing her. Every morning ere the McIntyre family were afoot a great bouquet of strange and beautiful flowers was brought down by a footman from the Hall to brighten their breakfast-table. Her slightest wish, however fantastic, was instantly satisfied, if human money or ingenuity could do it. When the frost lasted a stream was dammed and turned from its

course that it might flood two meadows, solely in order
that she might have a place upon which to skate. With
the thaw there came a groom every afternoon with a
sleek and beautiful mare in case Miss McIntyre should
care to ride. Everything went to show that she had
made a conquest of the recluse of the New Hall.

And she on her side played her part admirably. With
female adaptiveness she fell in with his humour, and
looked at the world through his eyes. Her talk was of
almshouses and free libraries, of charities and of
improvements. He had never a scheme to which she
could not add some detail making it more complete and
more effective. To Haw it seemed that at last he had
met a mind which was in absolute affinity with his own.
Here was a helpmate, who could not only follow, but
even lead him in the path which he had chosen.

Neither Robert nor his father could fail to see what
was going forward, but to the latter nothing could
possibly be more acceptable than a family tie which
should connect him, however indirectly, with a man of
vast fortune. The glamour of the gold bags had crept
over Robert also, and froze the remonstrance upon his
lips. It was very pleasant to have the handling of all this
wealth, even as a mere agent. Why should he do or say
what might disturb their present happy relations? It
was his sister's business, not his; and as to Hector
Spurling, he must take his chance as other men did. It
was obviously best not to move one way or the other in
the matter.

But to Robert himself, his work and his surroundings
were becoming more and more irksome. His joy in his
art had become less keen since he had known Raffles
Haw. It seemed so hard to toil and slave to earn such a

trifling sum, when money could really be had for the asking. It was true that he had asked for none, but large sums were for ever passing through his hands for those who were needy, and if he were needy himself his friend would surely not grudge it to him. So the Roman galleys still remained faintly outlined upon the great canvas, while Robert's days were spent either in the luxurious library at the Hall, or in strolling about the country listening to tales of trouble, and returning like a tweed-suited ministering angel to carry Raffles Haw's help to the unfortunate. It was not an ambitious life, but it was one which was very congenial to his weak and easy-going nature.

Robert had observed that fits of depression had frequently come upon the millionaire, and it had sometimes struck him that the enormous sums which he spent had possibly made a serious inroad into his capital, and that his mind was troubled as to the future. His abstracted manner, his clouded brow, and his bent head all spoke of a soul which was weighed down with care, and it was only in Laura's presence that he could throw off the load of his secret trouble. For five hours a day he buried himself in the laboratory and amused himself with his hobby, but it was one of his whims that no one, neither any of his servants, nor even Laura or Robert, should ever cross the threshold of that outlying building. Day after day he vanished into it, to reappear hours afterwards pale and exhausted, while the whirr of machinery and the smoke which streamed from his high chimney showed how considerable were the operations which he undertook single-handed.

"Could I not assist you in any way?" suggested Robert, as they sat together after luncheon in the smoking-room. "I am convinced that you over-try your strength. I should be so glad to help you, and I know a little of chemistry."

"Do you, indeed?" said Raffles Haw, raising his eyebrows. "I had no idea of that; it is very seldom that the artistic and the scientific faculties go together."

"I don't know that I have either particularly developed. But I have taken classes, and I worked for two years in the laboratory at Sir Josiah Mason's Institute."

"I am delighted to hear it," Haw replied with emphasis. "That may be of great importance to us. It is very possible — indeed, almost certain — that I shall avail myself of your offer of assistance, and teach you something of my chemical methods, which I may say differ considerably from those of the orthodox school. The time, however, is hardly ripe for that. What is it, Jones?"

"A note, sir."

The butler handed it in upon a silver salver. Haw broke the seal and ran his eye over it.

"Tut! tut! It is from Lady Morsley, asking me to the Lord-Lieutenant's ball. I cannot possibly accept. It is very kind of them, but I do wish they would leave me alone. Very well, Jones. I shall write. Do you know, Robert, I am often very unhappy."

He frequently called the young artist by his Christian name, especially in his more confidential moments.

"I have sometimes feared that you were," said the other sympathetically. "But how strange it seems, you who are yet young, healthy, with every faculty for enjoyment, and a millionaire."

"Ah, Robert," cried Haw, leaning back in his chair, and sending up thick blue wreaths from his pipe. "You have put your finger upon my trouble. If I were a millionaire I might be happy, but, alas, I am no millionaire!"

"Good heavens!" gasped Robert.

Cold seemed to shoot to his inmost soul as it flashed upon him that this was a prelude to a confession of impending bankruptcy, and that all this glorious life, all the excitement and the colour and change, were about to vanish into thin air.

"No millionaire!" he stammered.

"No, Robert; I am a billionaire — perhaps the only one in the world. That is what is on my mind, and why I am unhappy sometimes. I feel that I should spend this money — that I should put it in circulation — and yet it is so hard to do it without failing to do good — without doing positive harm. I feel my responsibility deeply. It weighs me down. Am I justified in continuing to live this quiet life when there are so many millions whom I might save and comfort if I could but reach them?"

Robert heaved a long sigh of relief.

"Perhaps you take too grave a view of your responsibilities," he said. "Everybody knows that the good which you have done is immense. What more could you desire? If you really wished to extend your benevolence further, there are organized charities everywhere which would be very glad of your help."

"I have the names of two hundred and seventy of them," Haw answered. "You must run your eye over them some time, and see if you can suggest any others. I send my annual mite to each of them. I don't think there is much room for expansion in that direction."

"Well, really you have done your share, and more than your share. I would settle down to lead a happy life, and think no more of the matter."

"I could not do that," Haw answered earnestly. "I have not been singled out to wield this immense power simply in order that I might lead a happy life. I can never believe that. Now, can you not use your imagination, Robert, and devise methods by which a man who has command of—well, let us say, for argument's sake, boundless wealth, could benefit mankind by it, without taking away any one's independence or in any way doing harm?"

"Well, really, now that I come to think of it, it is a very difficult problem," said Robert.

"Now I will submit a few schemes to you, and you may give me your opinion on them. Supposing that such a man were to buy ten square miles of ground here in Staffordshire, and were to build upon it a neat city, consisting entirely of clean, comfortable little four-roomed houses, furnished in a simple style, with shops and so forth, but no public-houses. Supposing, too, that he were to offer a house free to all the homeless folk, all the tramps, and broken men, and out-of-workers in Great Britain. Then, having collected them together, let him employ them, under fitting super-intendence, upon some colossal piece of work which would last for many years, and perhaps be of permanent value to humanity. Give them a good rate of pay, and let their hours of labour be reasonable, and those of recreation be pleasant. Might you not benefit them and benefit humanity at one stroke?"

"But what form of work could you devise which would employ so vast a number for so long a time, and yet not compete with an existing industry? To do the latter would simply mean to shift the misery from one class to another."

"Precisely so. I should compete with no one. What I

thought of doing was of sinking a shaft through the earth's crust, and of establishing rapid communication with the Antipodes. When you had got a certain distance down — how far is an interesting mathematical problem — the centre of gravity would be beneath you, presuming that your boring was not quite directed towards the centre, and you could then lay down rails and tunnel as if you were on the level."

Then for the first time it flashed into Robert McIntyre's head that his father's chance words were correct, and that he was in the presence of a madman. His great wealth had clearly turned his brain, and made him a monomaniac. He nodded indulgently, as when one humours a child.

"It would be very nice," he said. "I have heard, however, that the interior of the earth is molten, and your workmen would need to be Salamanders."

"The latest scientific data do not bear out the idea that the earth is so hot," answered Raffles Haw. "It is certain that the increased temperature in coal mines depends upon the barometric pressure. There are gases in the earth which may be ignited, and there are combustible materials as we see in the volcanoes; but if we came across anything of the sort in our borings, we could turn a river or two down the shaft, and get the better of it in that fashion."

"It would be rather awkward if the other end of your shaft came out under the Pacific Ocean," said Robert, choking down his inclination to laugh.

"I have had estimates and calculations from the first living engineers — French, English, and American. The point of exit of the tunnel could be calculated to the yard. That portfolio in the corner is full of sections, plans, and diagrams. I have agents employed in buying up land, and if all goes well, we may get to work in the autumn. That is one device which may produce results. Another is canal-cutting."

"Ah, there you would compete with the railways."

"You don't quite understand. I intend to cut canals through every neck of land where such a convenience would facilitate commerce. Such a scheme, when unaccompanied by any toll upon vessels, would, I think, be a very judicious way of helping the human race."

"And where, pray, would you cut the canals?" asked Robert.

"I have a map of the world here," Haw answered, rising, and taking one down from the paper-rack. "You see the blue pencil marks. Those are the points where I propose to establish communication. Of course, I should begin by the obvious duty of finishing the Panama business."

"Naturally." The man's lunacy was becoming more and more obvious, and yet there was such precision and coolness in his manner, that Robert found himself against his own reason endorsing and speculating over his plans.

"The Isthmus of Corinth also occurs to one. That, however, is a small matter, from either a financial or an engineering point of veiw. I propose, however, to make a junction here, through Kiel between the German Ocean and the Baltic. It saves, you will observe, the whole journey round the coast of Denmark, and would facilitate our trade with Germany and Russia. Another very obvious improvement is to join the Forth and the Clyde, so as to connect Leith with the Irish and American routes. You see the blue line?"

"Quite so."

"And we will have a little cutting here. It will run

from Uleaborg to Kem, and will connect the White Sea
with the Gulf of Bothnia. We must not allow our
sympathies to be insular, must we? Our little charities
should be cosmopolitan. We will try and give the good
people of Archangel a better outlet for their furs and
their tallow."

"But it will freeze."

"For six months in the year. Still, it will be something. Then we must do something for the East. It
would never do to overlook the East."

"It would certainly be an oversight," said Robert,
who was keenly alive to the comical side of the question.
Raffles Haw, however, in deadly earnest, sat scratching
away at his map with his blue pencil.

"Here is a point where we might be of some little
use. If we cut through from Batoum to the Kura River
we might tap the trade of the Caspian, and open up
communication with all the rivers which run into it.
You notice that they include a considerable tract of
country. Then, again, I think that we might venture
upon a little cutting between Beirut, on the Mediter-
ranean, and the upper waters of the Euphrates, which
would lead us into the Persian Gulf. Those are one or
two of the more obvious canals which might knit the
human race into a closer whole."

"Your plans are certainly stupendous," said Robert,
uncertain whether to laugh or to be awe-struck. "You
will cease to be a man, and become one of the great
forces of Nature, altering, moulding, and improving."

"That is precisely the view which I take of myself.
That is why I feel my responsibility so acutely."

"But surely if you will do all this you may rest. It is a
considerable programme."

"Not at all. I am a patriotic Briton, and I should like
to do something to leave my name in the annals of my

country. I should prefer, however, to do it after my own death, as anything in the shape of publicity and honour is very offensive to me. I have, therefore, put by eight hundred million in a place which shall be duly mentioned in my will, which I propose to devote to paying off the National Debt. I cannot see that any harm could arise from its extinction."

Robert sat staring, struck dumb by the audacity of the strange man's words.

"Then there is the heating of the soil. There is room for improvement there. You have no doubt read of the immense yields which have resulted in Jersey and elsewhere, from the running of hot-water pipes through the soil. The crops are trebled and quadrupled. I would propose to try the experiment upon a larger scale. We might possibly reserve the Isle of Man to serve as a pumping and heating station. The main pipes would run to England, Ireland, and Scotland, where they would subdivide rapidly until they formed a network two feet deep under the whole country. A pipe at distances of a yard would suffice for every purpose."

"I am afraid," suggested Robert, "that the water which left the Isle of Man warm might lose a little of its virtue before it reached Caithness, for example."

"There need not be any difficulty there. Every few miles a furnace might be arranged to keep up the temperature. These are a few of my plans for the future, Robert, and I shall want the co-operation of disinterested men like yourself in all of them. But how brightly the sun shines, and how sweet the country side looks! The world is very beautiful, and I should like to leave it happier than I found it. Let us walk out together, Robert, and you will tell me of any fresh cases where I may be of assistance."

IX

A NEW DEPARTURE

WHATEVER GOOD Mr. Raffles Haw's wealth did to the world, there could be no doubt that there were cases where it did harm. The very contemplation and thought of it had upon many a disturbing and mischievous effect. Especially was this the case with the old gunmaker. From being merely a querelous and grasping man, he had now become bitter, brooding, and dangerous. Week by week, as he saw the tide of wealth flow as it were through his very house without being able to divert the smallest rill to nourish his own fortunes, he became more wolfiish and more hungry-eyed. He spoke less of his own wrongs, but he brooded more, and would stand for hours on Tamfield Hill looking down at the great palace beneath, as a thirst-stricken man might gaze at the desert mirage.

He had worked, and peeped, and pried, too, until there were points upon which he knew more than either his son or his daughter.

"I suppose that you still don't know where your friend gets his money?" he remarked to Robert one morning, as they walked together through the village.

"No, father, I do not. I only know that he spends it very well."

"Well!" snarled the old man. "Yes, very well! He has helped every tramp and slut and worthless vagabond over the countryside, but he will not advance a pound, even on the best security, to help a respectable business man to fight against misfortune."

"My dear father, I really cannot argue with you about it," said Robert. "I have already told you more than once what I think. Mr. Haw's object is to help those who are destitute. He looks upon us as his equals, and would not presume to patronize us, or to act as if we could not help ourselves. It would be a humiliation to us to take his money."

"Pshaw! Besides, it is only a question of an advance, and advances are made every day among business men. How can you talk such nonsense, Robert?"

Early as it was, his son could see from his excited, quarrelsome manner that the old man had been drinking. The habit had grown upon him of late, and it was seldom now that he was entirely sober.

"Mr. Raffles Haw is the best judge," said Robert coldly. "If he earns the money, he has a right to spend it as he likes."

"And how does he earn it? You don't know, Robert. You don't know that you aren't aiding and abetting a felony when you help him to fritter it away. Was ever so much money earned in an honest fashion? I tell you there never was. I tell you, also, that lumps of gold are no more to that man than chunks of coal to the miners over yonder. He could build his house of them and think nothing of it."

"I know that he is very rich, father. I think, however, that he has an extravagant way of talking sometimes, and that his imagination carries him away. I have heard him talk of plans which the richest man upon earth could not possibly hope to carry through."

"Don't you make any mistake, my son. Your poor old father isn't quite a fool, though he is only an honest broken merchant." He looked up sideways at his son with a wink and a most unpleasant leer. "Where there's money I can smell it. There's money there, and heaps of it. It's my belief that he is the richest man in the world, though how he came to be so I should not like to guarantee. I'm not quite blind yet, Robert. Have you seen the weekly waggon?"

"The weekly waggon!"

"Yes, Robert. You see I can find some news for you yet. It is due this morning. Every Saturday morning you will see the waggon come in. Why, here it is now, as I am a living man, coming round the curve."

Robert glanced back and saw a great heavy waggon drawn by two strong horses lumbering slowly along the road which led to the New Hall. From the efforts of the animals and its slow pace the contents seemed to be of great weight.

"Just you wait here," old McIntyre cried, plucking at his son's sleeve with his thin bony hand. "Wait here and see it pass. Then we will watch what becomes of it."

They stood by the side of the road until it came abreast of them. The waggon was covered with tarpaulin sheetings in front and at the sides, but behind some glimpse could be caught of the contents. They consisted, as far as Robert could see, of a number of packets of the same shape, each about two feet long and six inches high, arranged symmetrically upon the top of each other. Each packet was surrounded by a covering of coarse sacking.

"What do you think of that?" asked old McIntyre triumphantly as the load creaked past.

"Why, father? What do you make of it?"

"I have watched it, Robert — I have watched it every Saturday, and I had my chance of looking a little deeper into it. You remember the day when the elm blew down, and the road was blocked until they could saw it in two. That was on a Saturday, and the waggon came to a stand until they could clear a way for it. I was there, Robert, and I saw my chance. I strolled behind the waggon, and I placed my hands upon one of those packets. They look small, do they not? It would take a strong man to lift one. They are heavy, Robert, heavy, and hard with the hardness of metal. I tell you, boy, that that waggon is loaded with gold."

"Gold!"

"With solid bars of gold, Robert. But come into the plantation and we shall see what becomes of it."

They passed through the lodge gates, behind the waggon, and then wandered off among the fir-trees until they gained a spot where they could command a view. The load had halted, not in front of the house, but at the door of the out-building with the chimney. A staff of stablemen and footmen were in readiness, who proceeded to swiftly unload and to carry the packages through the door. It was the first time that Robert had ever seen any one save the master of the house enter the laboratory. No sign was seen of him now, however, and in half an hour the contents had all been safely stored and the waggon had driven briskly away.

"I cannot understand it, father," said Robert thoughtfully, as they resumed their walk. "Supposing that your supposition is correct, who would send him such quantities of gold, and where could it come from?"

"Ha, you have to come to the old man after all!" chuckled his companion. "I can see the little game. It is clear enough to me. There are two of them in it, you understand. The other one gets the gold. Never mind how, but we will hope that there is no harm. Let us suppose, for example, that they have found a marvellous mine, where you can just shovel it out like clay from a pit. Well, then, he sends it on to this one, and he has his furnaces and his chemicals, and he refines and purifies it and makes it fit to sell. That's my explanation of it, Robert. Eh, has the old man put his finger on it?"

"But if that were true, father, the gold must go back again."

"So it does, Robert, but a little at a time. Ha, ha! I've had my eyes open, you see. Every night it goes down in a small cart, and is sent on to London by the 7.40. Not in bars this time, but done up in iron-bound chests. I've seen them, boy, and I've had this hand upon them."

"Well," said the young man thoughtfully, "maybe you are right. It is possible that you are right."

While father and son were prying into his secrets Raffles Haw had found his way to Elmdene, where Laura sat reading the *Queen* by the fire.

"I am so sorry," she said, throwing down her paper and springing to her feet. "They are all out except me. But I am sure that they won't be long. I expect Robert every moment."

"I would rather speak with you alone," answered Raffles Haw quietly. "Pray sit down, for I wanted to have a little chat with you."

Laura resumed her seat with a flush upon her cheeks and a quickening of the breath. She turned her face away and gazed into the fire; but there was a sparkle in her eyes which was not caught from the leaping flames.

"Do you remember the first time that we met, Miss McIntyre?" he asked, standing on the rug and looking down at her dark hair, and the beautifully feminine curve of her ivory neck.

"As if it were yesterday," she answered in her sweet mellow tones.

"Then you must also remember the wild words that I said when we parted. It was very foolish of me. I am sure that I am most sorry if I frightened or disturbed you, but I have been a very solitary man for a long time, and I have dropped into a bad habit of thinking aloud. Your voice, you face, your manner, were all so like my ideal of a true woman, loving, faithful, and sympathetic, that I could not help wondering whether, if I were a poor man, I might ever hope to win the affection of such a one."

"Your good opinion, Mr. Raffles Haw, is very dear to me," said Laura. "I assure you that I was not frightened, and that there is no need to apologize for what was really a compliment."

"Since then I have found," he continued, "that all that I had read upon your face was true. That your mind is indeed that of the true woman, full of the noblest and sweetest qualities which human nature can aspire to. You know that I am a man of fortune, but I wish you to dismiss that consideration from your mind. Do you think from what you know of my character that you could be happy as my wife, Laura?"

She made no answer, but still sat with her head turned away and her sparkling eyes fixed upon the fire. One little foot from under her skirt tapped nervously upon the rug.

"It is only right that you should know a little more about me before you decide. There is, however, little to know. I am an orphan, and, as far as I know, without a relation upon earth. My father was a respectable man, a country surgeon in Wales, and he brought me up to his own profession. Before I had passed my examinations, however, he died and left me a small annuity. I had conceived a great liking for the subjects of chemistry and electricity, and instead of going on with my medical work I devoted myself entirely to these studies, and eventually built myself a laboratory where I could follow out my own researches. At about this time I came into a very large sum of money, so large as to make me feel that a vast responsibility rested upon me in the use which I made of it. After some thought I determined to build a large house in a quiet part of the country, not too far from a great centre. There I could be in touch with the world, and yet would have quiet and leisure to mature the schemes which were in my head. As it chanced, I chose Tamfield as my site. All that remains now is to carry out the plans which I have made, and to endeavour to lighten the earth of some of the misery and injustice which weigh it down. I again ask you, Laura, will you throw in your lot with mine, and help me in the life's work which lies before me?"

Laura looked up at him, at his stringy figure, his pale face, his keen, yet gentle eyes. Somehow as she looked there seemed to form itself beside him some shadow of Hector Spurling, the manly features, the clear, firm mouth, the frank manner. Now, in the very moment of her triumph, it sprang clearly up in her mind how at the hour of their ruin he had stood firmly by them, and had loved the penniless girl as tenderly as the heiress to fortune. That last embrace at the door, too, came back to her, and she felt his lips warm upon her own.

"I am very much honoured, Mr. Haw," she stammered, "but this is so sudden. I have not had time to think. I do not know what to say."

"Do not let me hurry you," he cried earnestly. "I beg that you will think well over it. I shall come again for my answer. When shall I come? To-night?"

"Yes, come to-night."

"Then, adieu. Believe me that I think more highly of you for your hesitation. I shall live in hope." He raised her hand to his lips, and left her to her own thoughts.

But what those thoughts were did not long remain in doubt. Dimmer and dimmer grew the vision of the distant sailor face, clearer and clearer the image of the vast palace, of the queenly power, of the diamonds, the gold, the ambitious future. It all lay at her feet, waiting to be picked up. How could she have hesitated, even for a moment? She rose, and, walking over to her desk, she took out a sheet of paper and an envelope. The latter she addressed to Lieutenant Spurling, H.M.S. *Active,* Gibraltar. The note cost some little trouble, but at last she got it worded to her mind.

"DEAR HECTOR," she said — "I am convinced that your father has never entirely approved of our engagement, otherwise he would not have thrown obstacles in the way of our marriage. I am sure, too, that since my poor father's misfortune it is only your own sense of honour and feeling of duty which have kept you true to me, and that you would have done infinitely better had you never seen me. I cannot bear, Hector, to allow you to imperil your future for my sake, and I have determined, after thinking well over the matter, to release you from our boy and girl engagement, so that you may be entirely free in every way. It is possible that you may think it unkind of me to do this now, but I am quite sure, dear Hector, that when you are an admiral and a very distinguished man, you will look back at this, and you will see that I have been a true friend to you, and have prevented you from making a false step early in your career. For myself, whether I marry or not, I have determined to devote the remainder of my life to trying to do good, and to leaving the world happier than I found it. Your father is very well, and gave us a capital sermon last Sunday. I enclose the bank-note which you asked me to keep for you. Good-bye, for ever, dear Hector, and believe me when I say that, come what may, I am ever your true friend,

"LAURA S. MCINTYRE."

She had hardly sealed her letter before her father and Robert returned. She closed the door behind them, and made them a little curtsey.

"I await my family's congratulations," she said, with her head in the air. "Mr. Raffles Haw has been here, and he has asked me to be his wife."

"The deuce he did!" cried the old man. "And you said — ?"

"I am to see him again."

"And you will say — ?"

"I will accept him."

"You were always a good girl, Laura," said old McIntyre, standing on his tiptoes to kiss her.

"But Laura, Laura, how about Hector?" asked Robert in mild remonstrance.

"Oh, I have written to him," his sister answered carelessly. "I wish you would be good enough to post the letter."

"If you will be good enough to accompany me to the laboratory . . ."

X

THE GREAT SECRET

AND SO Laura McIntyre became duly engaged to Raffles Haw, and old McIntyre grew even more hungry-looking as he felt himself a step nearer to the source of wealth, while Robert thought less of work than ever, and never gave as much as a thought to the great canvas which still stood, dust-covered, upon his easel. Haw gave Laura an engagement ring of old gold, with a great blazing diamond bulging out of it. There was little talk about the matter, however, for it was Haw's wish that all should be done very quietly. Nearly all his evenings were spent at Elmdene, where he and Laura would build up the most colossal schemes of philanthropy for the future. With a map stretched out on the table in front of them, these two young people would, as it were, hover over the world, planning, devising, and improving.

"Bless the girl!" said old McIntyre to his son; "she speaks about it as if she were born to millions. Maybe, when once she is married, she won't be so ready to chuck her money into every mad scheme that her husband can think of."

"Laura is greatly changed," Robert answered; "she has grown much more serious in her ideas."

"You wait a bit!" sniggered his father. "She is a good girl, is Laura, and she knows what she is about. She's not a girl to let her old dad go to the wall if she can set him right. It's a pretty state of things," he added bitterly: "here's my daughter going to marry a man who thinks no more of gold than I used to of gun-metal; and here's my son going about with all the money he cares to ask for to help every ne'er-do-well in Stafford-shire; and here's their father, who loved them and cared for them, and brought them both up, without money enough very often to buy a bottle of brandy. I don't know what your poor dear mother would have thought of it."

"You have only to ask for what you want."

"Yes, as if I were a five-year-old child. But I tell you, Robert, I'll have my rights, and if I can't get them one way I will another. I won't be treated as if I were no one. And there's one thing: if I am to be this man's pa-in-law, I'll want to know something about him and his money first. We may be poor, but we are honest. I'll up to the Hall now, and have it out with him." He seized his hat and stick and made for the door.

"No, no, father," cried Robert, catching him by the sleeve. "You had better leave the matter alone. Mr. Haw is a very sensitive man. He would not like to be examined upon such a point. It might lead to a serious quarrel. I beg that you will not go."

"I am not to be put off for ever," snarled the old man, who had been drinking heavily. "I'll put my foot down now, once and for ever." He tugged at his sleeve to free himself from his son's grasp.

"At least you shall not go without Laura knowing. I will call her down, and we shall have her opinion."

"Oh, I don't want to have any scenes," said

McIntyre sulkily, relaxing his efforts. He lived in dread of his daughter, and at his worst moments the mention of her name would serve to restrain him.

"Besides," said Robert, "I have not the slightest doubt that Raffles Haw will see the necessity for giving us some sort of explanation before matters go further. He must understand that we have some claim now to be taken into his confidence."

He had hardly spoken where there was a tap at the door, and the man of whom they were speaking walked in.

"Good-morning, Mr. McIntyre," said he. "Robert, would you mind stepping up to the Hall with me? I want to have a little business chat." He looked serious, like a man who is carrying out something which he has well weighed.

They walked up together with hardly a word on either side. Raffles Haw was absorbed in his own thoughts. Robert felt expectant and nervous, for he knew that something of importance lay before him. The winter had almost passed now, and the first young shoots were beginning to peep out timidly in the face of the wind and the rain of an English March. The snows were gone, but the countryside looked bleaker and drearier, all shrouded in the haze from the damp, sodden meadows.

"By the way, Robert," said Raffles Haw suddenly, as they walked up the Avenue. "Has your great Roman picture gone to London?"

"I have not finished it yet."

"But I know that you are a quick worker. You must be nearly at the end of it."

"No, I am afraid that it has not advanced much since

you saw it. For one thing, the light has not been very good."

Raffles Haw said nothing, but a pained expression flashed over his face. When they reached the house he led the way through the museum. Two great metal cases were lying on the floor.

"I have made a small addition there to the gem collection," he remarked as he passed. "They only arrived last night, and I have not opened them yet, but I am given to understand from the letters and invoices that there are some fine specimens. We might arrange them this afternoon, if you care to assist me. Let us go into the smoking-room now."

He threw himself down into a settee, and motioned Robert into the arm-chair in front of him.

"Light a cigar," he said. "Press the spring if there is any refreshment which you would like. Now, my dear Robert, confess to me in the first place that you have often thought me mad."

The charge was so direct and so true that the young artist hesitated, hardly knowing how to answer.

"My dear boy, I do not blame you. It was the most natural thing in the world. I should have looked upon anyone as a madman who had talked to me as I have talked to you. But for all that, Robert, you were wrong, and I have never yet in our conversations proposed any scheme which it was not well within my power to carry out. I tell you in all sober earnest that the amount of my income is limited only by my desire, and that all the bankers and financiers combined could not furnish the sums which I can put forward without an effort."

"I have had ample proof of your immense wealth," said Robert.

"And you are very naturally curious as to how that

wealth was obtained. Well, I can tell you one thing. The money is perfectly clean. I have robbed no one, cheated no one, sweated no one, ground no one down in the gaining of it. I can read your father's eye, Robert. I can see that he has done me an injustice in this matter. Well, perhaps he is not to be blamed. Perhaps I also might think uncharitable things if I were in his place. But that is why I now give an explanation to you, Robert, and not to him. You, at least, have trusted me, and you have a right, before I become one of your family, to know all that I can tell you. Laura also has trusted me, but I know well that she is content still to trust me."

"I would not intrude upon your secrets, Mr. Haw," said Robert, "but of course I cannot deny that I should be very proud and pleased if you cared to confide them to me."

"And I will. Not all. I do not think that I shall ever, while I live, tell all. But I shall leave directions behind me so that when I die you may be able to carry on my unfinished work. I shall tell you where those directions are to be found. In the meantime, you must be content to learn the effects which I produce without knowing every detail as to the means."

Robert settled himself down in his chair and concentrated his attention upon his companion's words, while Haw bent forward his eager, earnest face, like a man who knows the value of the words which he is saying.

"You are already aware," he remarked, "that I have devoted a great deal of energy and of time to the study of chemistry."

"So you told me."

"I commenced my studies under a famous English

chemist, I continued them under the best man in France, and I completed them in the most celebrated laboratory of Germany. I was not rich, but my father had left me enough to keep me comfortably, and by living economically I had a sum at my command which enabled me to carry out my studies in a very complete way. When I returned to England I built myself a laboratory in a quiet country place where I could work without distraction or interruption. There I began a series of investigations which soon took me into regions of science to which none of the three famous men who taught me had ever penetrated.

"You say, Robert, that you have some slight knowledge of chemistry, and you will find it easier to follow what I say. Chemistry is to a large extent an empirical science, and the chance experiment may lead to greater results than could, with our present data, be derived from the closest study or the keenest reasoning. The most important chemical discoveries from the first manufacture of glass to the whitening and refining of sugar have all been due to some happy chance which might have befallen a mere dabbler as easily as a deep student.

"Well, it was to such a chance that my own great discovery — perhaps the greatest that the world has seen — was due, though I may claim the credit of having originated the line of thought which led up to it. I had frequently speculated as to the effect which powerful currents of electricity exercise upon any substance through which they are poured for a considerable time. I did not here mean such feeble currents as are passed along a telegraph wire, but I mean the highest possible developments. Well, I tried a series of experiments upon this point. I found that in liquids, and in compounds, the force had a disintegrating effect. The well-known experiment of the electrolysis of water will, of course, occur to you. But I found that in the case of elemental solids the effect was a remarkable one. The element slowly decreased in weight, without perceptibly altering in composition. I hope that I make myself clear to you?"

"I follow you entirely," said Robert, deeply interested in his companion's narrative.

"I tried upon several elements, and always with the same result. In every case an hour's current would produce a perceptible loss of weight. My theory at that stage was that there was a loosening of the molecules caused by the electric fluid, and that a certain number of these molecules were shed off like an impalpable dust, all round the lump of earth or of metal, which remained, of course, the lighter by their loss. I had entirely accepted this theory, when a very remarkable chance led me to completely alter my opinions.

"I had one Saturday night fastened a bar of bismuth in a clamp, and had attached it on either side to an electric wire, in order to observe what effect the current would have upon it. I had been testing each metal in turn, exposing them to the influence for from one to two hours. I had just got everything in position, and had completed my connection, when I received a telegram to say that John Stillingfleet, an old chemist in London with whom I had been on terms of intimacy, was dangerously ill, and had expressed a wish to see me. The last train was due to leave in twenty minutes, and I lived a good mile from the station. I thrust a few things into a bag, locked my laboratory, and ran as hard as I could to catch it.

"It was not until I was in London that it suddenly

occurred to me that I had neglected to shut off the current, and that it would continue to pass through the bar of bismuth until the batteries were exhausted. The fact, however, seemed to be of small importance, and I dismissed it from my mind. I was detained in London until the Tuesday night, and it was Wednesday morning before I got back to my work. As I unlocked the laboratory door my mind reverted to the uncompleted experiment, and it struck me that in all probability my piece of bismuth would have been entirely disintegrated and reduced to its primitive molecules. I was utterly unprepared for the truth.

"When I approached the table I found, sure enough, that the bar of metal had vanished, and that the clamp was empty. Having noted the fact, I was about to turn away to something else, when my attention was attracted to the fact that the table upon which the clamp stood was starred over with little patches of some liquid silvery matter, which lay in single drops or coalesced into little pools. I had a very distinct recollection of having thoroughly cleared the table before beginning my experiment, so that this substance had been deposited there since I had left for London. Much interested, I very carefully collected it all into one vessel, and examined it minutely. There could be no question as to what it was. It was the purest mercury, and gave no response to any test for bismuth.

"I at once grasped the fact that chance had placed in my hands a chemical discovery of the very first importance. If bismuth were, under certain conditions, to be subjected to the action of electricity, it would begin by losing weight, and would finally be transformed into mercury. I had broken down the partition which separated two elements.

"But the process would be a constant one. It would presumably prove to be a general law, and not an isolated fact. If bismuth turned into mercury, what would mercury turn into? There would be no rest for me until I had solved the question. I renewed the exhausted batteries and passed the current through a bowl of quicksilver. For sixteen hours I sat watching the metal, marking how it slowly seemed to curdle, to grow firmer, to lose its silvery glitter and to take a dull yellow hue. When I at last picked it up in a forceps, and threw it upon the table, it had lost every characteristic of mercury, and had obviously become another metal. A few simple tests were enough to show me that this other metal was platinum.

"Now, to a chemist, there was something very suggestive in the order in which these changes had been effected. Perhaps you can see the relation, Robert, which they bear to each other?"

"No, I cannot say that I do."

Robert had sat listening to this strange statement with parted lips and staring eyes.

"I will show you. Speaking atomically, bismuth is the heaviest of the metals. Its atomic weight is 210. The next in weight is lead, 207, then comes mercury at 200. Possibly the long period during which the current had acted in my absence had reduced the bismuth to lead and the lead in turn to mercury. Now platinum stands at 197.5, and it was accordingly the next metal to be produced by the continued current. Do you see now?"

"It is quite clear."

"And then there came the inference, which sent my heart into my mouth and caused my head to swim round. Gold is the next in the series. Its atomic weight is 197. I remembered now, and for the first time understood why it was always lead and mercury which were mentioned by the old alchemists as being the two metals which might be used in their calling. With fingers which trembled with excitement I adjusted the wires again, and in little more than an hour — for the length of the process was always in proportion to the difference in the metals — I had before me a knob of ruddy crinkled metal, which answered to every reaction for gold.

"Well, Robert, this is a long story, but I think that you will agree with me that its importance justifies me in going into detail. When I had satisfied myself that I had really manufactured gold I cut the nugget in two. One half I sent to a jeweller and worker in precious metals, with whom I had some slight acquaintance, asking him to report upon the quality of the metal. With the other half I continued my series of experiments, and reduced it in successive stages through all the long series of metals, through silver and zinc and manganese, until I brought it to lithium, which is the lighest of all."

"And what did it turn to then?" asked Robert.

"Then came what to chemists is likely to be the most interesting portion of my discovery. It turned to a greyish fine powder, which powder gave no further results, however much I might treat it with electricity. And that powder is the base of all things; it is the mother of all the elements; it is, in short, the substance whose existence has been recently surmised by a leading chemist, and which has been christened protyle by him. I am the discoverer of the great law of the electrical transposition of the metals, and I am the first to demonstrate protyle, so that, I think, Robert, if all

my schemes in other directions come to nothing, my
name is at least likely to live in the chemical world.

"There is not very much more for me to tell you. I
had my nugget back from my friend the jeweller,
confirming my opinion as to its nature and its quality. I
soon found several methods by which the process might
be simplified, and especially a modification of the
ordinary electric current, which was very much more
effective. Having made a certain amount of gold, I
disposed of it for a sum which enabled me to buy
improved materials and stronger batteries. In this way
I enlarged my operations until at last I was in a position
to build this house and to have a laboratory where I
could carry out my work on a much larger scale. As I
said before, I can now state with all truth that the
amount of my income is only limited by my desires."

"It is wonderful!" gasped Robert. "It is like a fairy
tale. But with this great discovery in your mind you
must have been sorely tempted to confide it to others."

"I thought well over it. I gave it every consideration.
It was obvious to me that if my invention were made
public, its immediate result would be to deprive the
present precious metals of all their special value. Some
other substance — amber, we will say, or ivory — would
be chosen as a medium for barter, and gold would be
inferior to brass, as being heavier and yet not so hard.
No one would be the better for such a consummation as
that. Now, if I retained my secret, and used it with
wisdom, I might make myself the greatest benefactor to
mankind that has ever lived. Those were the chief
reasons, and I trust that they are not dishonourable
ones, which led me to form the resolution, which I have
to-day for the first time broken."

"But your secret is safe with me," cried Robert. "My lips shall be sealed until I have your permission to speak."

"If I had not known that I could trust you I should have withheld it from your knowledge. And now, my dear Robert, theory is very weak work, and practice is infinitely more interesting. I have given you more than enough of the first. If you will be good enough to accompany me to the laboratory I shall give you a little of the latter."

XI

A Chemical Demonstration

R AFFLES HAW led the way through the front door, and crossing over the gravelled drive pushed open the outer door of the laboratory — the same through which the McIntyres had seen the packages conveyed from the waggon. On passing through it Robert found that they were not really within the building, but merely in a large bare ante-chamber, around the walls of which were stacked the very objects which had aroused his curiosity and his father's speculations. All mystery had gone from them now, however, for while some were still wrapped in their sackcloth coverings, others had been undone, and revealed themselves as great pigs of lead.

"There is my raw material," said Raffles Haw carelessly, nodding at the heap. "Every Saturday I have a waggon-load sent up, which serves me for a week, but we shall need to work double tides when Laura and I are married, and we get our great schemes under way. I have to be very careful about the quality of the lead, for, of course, every impurity is reproduced in the gold."

A heavy iron door led into the inner chamber. Haw unlocked it, but only to disclose a second one about five feet further on.

"This flooring is all disconnected at night," he remarked. "I have no doubt that there is a good deal of gossip in the servants'-hall about this sealed chamber, so I have to guard myself against some inquisitive ostler or too adventurous butler."

The inner door admitted them into the laboratory, a high, bare, whitewashed room with a glass roof. At one end was the furnace and boiler, the iron mouth of which was closed, though the fierce red light beat through the cracks, and a dull roar sounded through the building. On either side innumerable huge Leyden jars stood ranged in rows, tier topping tier, while above them were columns of Voltaic cells. Robert's eyes, as he glanced around, lit on vast wheels, complicated networks of wire, stands, test-tubes, coloured bottles, graduated glasses, Bunsen burners, porcelain insulators, and all the varied *débris* of a chemical and electrical workshop.

"Come across here," said Raffles Haw, picking his way among the heaps of metal, the coke, the packing-cases, and the carboys of acid. "Yours is the first foot except my own which has ever penetrated to this room since the workmen left it. My servants carry the lead into the anteroom, but come no further. The furnace can be cleaned and stoked from without. I employ a fellow to do nothing else. Now take a look in here."

He threw open a door on the further side, and motioned to the young artist to enter. The latter stood silent with one foot over the threshold, staring in amazement around him. The room, which may have been some thirty feet square, was paved and walled with gold. Great brick-shaped ingots, closely packed, covered the whole floor, while on every side they were reared up in compact barriers to the very ceiling. The single electric lamp which lighted the windowless chamber struck a dull, murky, yellow light from the vast piles of precious metal, and gleamed ruddily upon the golden floor.

"This is my treasure house," remarked the owner. "You see that I have rather an accumulation just now. My imports have been exceeding my exports. You can understand that I have other and more important duties even than the making of gold, just now. This is where I store my output until I am ready to send it off. Every night almost I am in the habit of sending a case of it to London. I employ seventeen brokers in its sale. Each thinks that he is the only one, and each is dying to know where I can get such large quantities of virgin gold. They say that it is the purest which comes into the market. The popular theory is, I believe, that I am a middleman acting on behalf of some new South African mine, which wishes to keep its whereabouts a secret. What value would you put upon the gold in this chamber? It ought to be worth something, for it represents nearly a week's work."

"Something fabulous, I have no doubt," said Robert, glancing round at the yellow barriers. "Shall I say a hundred and fifty thousand pounds?"

"Oh dear me, it is surely worth very much more than that," cried Raffles Haw, laughing. "Let me see. Suppose that we put it at three ten an ounce, which is nearly ten shillings under the mark. That makes, roughly, fifty-six pounds for a pound in weight. Now each of these ingots weighs thirty-six pounds, which brings their value to two thousand and a few odd pounds. There are five hundred ingots on each of these three sides of the room, but on the fourth there are only three hundred, on account of the door, but there cannot be less than two hundred on the floor, which gives us a rough total of two thousand ingots. So you see, my dear boy, that any broker who could get the contents of this chamber for four million pounds would be doing a nice little stroke of business."

"And a week's work!" gasped Robert. "It makes my head swim."

"You will follow me now when I repeat that none of the great schemes which I intend to simultaneously set in motion are at all likely to languish for want of funds. Now come into the laboratory with me and see how it is done."

In the centre of the workroom was an instrument like a huge vice, with two large brass-coloured plates, and a great steel screw for bringing them together. Numerous wires ran into these metal plates, and were attached at the other end to the rows of dynamic machines. Beneath was a glass stand, which was hollowed out in the centre into a succession of troughs.

"You will soon understand all about it," said Raffles Haw, throwing off his coat, and pulling on a smoke-stained and dirty linen jacket. "We must first stoke up a little." He put his weight on a pair of great bellows, and an answering roar came from the furnance. "That will do. The more heat the more electric force, and the quicker our task. Now for the lead! Just give me a hand in carrying it."

They lifted a dozen of the pigs of lead from the floor on to the glass stand, and having adjusted the plates on either side, Haw screwed up the handle so as to hold them in position.

"It used in the early days to be a slow process," he remarked; "but now that I have immense facilities for my work it takes a very short time. I have now only to complete the connection in order to begin."

He took hold of a long glass lever which projected from among the wires, and drew it downwards. A sharp click was heard, followed by a loud, sparkling, crackling noise. Great spurts of flame sprang from the two electrodes, and the mass of lead was surrounded by an aureole of golden sparks, which hissed and snapped like pistol-shots. The air was filled with the peculiar acid smell of ozone.

"The power there is immense," said Raffles Haw, superintending the process, with his watch upon the palm of his hand. "It would reduce an organic substance to protyle instantly. It is well to understand the mechanism thoroughly, for any mistake might be a grave matter for the operator. You are dealing with gigantic forces. But you perceive that the lead is already beginning to turn."

Silvery dew-like drops had indeed begun to form upon the dull-coloured mass, and to drop with a tinkle and splash into the glass troughs. Slowly the lead melted away, like an icicle in the sun, the electrodes ever closing upon it as it contracted, until they came together in the centre, and a row of pools of quicksilver had taken the place of the solid metal. Two smaller electrodes were plunged into the mercury, which gradually curdled and solidified, until it had resumed the solid form, with a yellowish brassy shimmer.

"What lies in the moulds now is platinum," remarked Raffles Haw. "We must take it from the troughs and refix it in the large electrodes. So! Now we turn on the current again. You see that it gradually takes a darker and richer tint. Now I think that it is perfect." He drew up the lever, removed the electrodes, and there lay a dozen bricks of ruddy sparkling gold.

"You see, according to our calculations, our morning's work has been worth twenty-four thousand pounds, and it has not taken us more than twenty minutes," remarked the alchemist, as he picked up the newly-made ingots, and threw them down among the others.

"We will devote one of them to experiment," said he, leaving the last standing upon the glass insulator. "To the world it would seem an expensive demonstration which cost two thousand pounds, but our standard, you see, is a different one. Now you will see me run through the whole gamut of metallic nature."

First of all men after the discoverer, Robert saw the gold mass, when the electrodes were again applied to it, change swiftly and successfully to barium, to tin, to silver, to copper, to iron. He saw the long white electric sparks change to crimson with the strontium, to purple with the potassium, to yellow with the manganese. Then, finally, after a hundred transformations, it disintegrated before his eyes, and lay as a little mound of fluffy grey dust upon the glass table.

"And this is protyle," said Haw, passing his fingers through it. "The chemist of the future may resolve it into further constituents, but to me it is the Ultima Thule."

"And now, Robert," he continued, after a pause, "I have shown you enough to enable you to understand something of my system. This is the great secret. It is the secret which endows the man who knows it with such a universal power as no man has ever enjoyed since the world was made. This secret it is the dearest wish of my heart to use for good, and I swear to you,

Robert McIntyre, that if I thought it would tend to anything but good I would have done with it for ever. No, I would neither use it myself nor would any other man learn it from my lips. I swear it by all that is holy and solemn!"

His eyes flashed as he spoke, and his voice quivered with emotion. Standing, pale and lanky, amid his electrodes and his retorts, there was still something majestic about this man, who, amid all his stupendous good fortune, could still keep his moral sense undazzled by the glitter of his gold. Robert's weak nature had never before realized the strength which lay in those thin, firm lips and earnest eyes.

"Surely in your hands, Mr. Haw, nothing but good can come of it," he said.

"I hope not—I pray not—most earnestly do I pray not. I have done for you, Robert, what I might not have done for my own brother had I one, and I have done it because I believe and hope that you are a man who would not use this power, should you inherit it, for selfish ends. But even now I have not told you all. There is one link which I have withheld from you, and which shall be withheld from you while I live. But look at this chest, Robert."

He led him to a great iron-clamped chest which stood in the corner, and, throwing it open, he took from it a small case of carved ivory.

"Inside this," he said, "I have left a paper which makes clear anything which is still hidden from you. Should anything happen to me you will always be able to inherit my powers, and to continue my plans by following the directions which are there expressed. And now," he continued, throwing his casket back again into the box, "I shall frequently require your help, but

I do not think it will be necessary this morning. I have already taken up too much of your time. If you are going back to Elmdene I wish that you would tell Laura that I shall be with her in the afternoon."

A FAMILY JAR

A ND SO the great secret was out, and Robert walked
home with his head in a whirl, and the blood
tingling in his veins. He had shivered as he
came up at the damp cold of wind and the sight of the
mist-mottled landscape. That was all gone now. His
own thoughts tinged everything with sunshine, and he
felt inclined to sing and dance as he walked down the
muddy, deeply-rutted country lane. Wonderful had
been the fate allotted to Raffles Haw, but surely hardly
less important that which had come upon himself. He
was the sharer of the alchemist's secret, and the heir to
an inheritance which combined a wealth greater than
that of monarchs, to a freedom such as monarchs
cannot enjoy. This was a destiny indeed! A thousand
gold-tinted visions of his future life rose up before him,
and in fancy he already sat high above the human race,
with prostrate thousands imploring his aid, or thanking
him for his benevolence.

How sordid seemed the untidy garden, with its
scraggy bushes and gaunt elm-trees! How mean the
plain brick front, with green wooden porch! It had
always offended his artistic sense, but now it was
obtrusive in its ugliness. The plain room, too, with the
American leather chairs, the dull-coloured carpet, and

the patchwork rug, he felt a loathing for it all. The only pretty thing in it, upon which his eyes could rest with satisfaction, was his sister, as she leaned back in her chair by the fire with her white, clear beautiful face outlined against the dark background.

"Do you know, Robert," she said, glancing up at him from under her long black lashes, "Papa grows unendurable. I have had to speak very plainly to him, and to make him understand that I am marrying for my own benefit and not for his."

"Where is he, then?"

"I don't know. At the Three Pigeons, no doubt. He spends most of his time there now. He flew off in a passion, and talked such nonsense about marriage settlements, and forbidding the banns, and so on. His notion of a marriage settlement appears to be a settlement upon the bride's father. He should wait quietly, and see what can be done for him."

"I think, Laura, that we must make a good deal of allowance for him," said Robert earnestly. "I have noticed a great change in him lately. I don't think he is himself at all. I must get some medical advice. But I have been up at the Hall this morning."

"Have you? Have you seen Raffles? Did he send anything for me?"

"He said that he would come down when he had finished his work."

"But what is the matter, Robert?" cried Laura, with the swift perception of womanhood. "You are flushed, and your eyes are shining, and really you look quite handsome. Raffles has been telling you something! What was it? Oh, I know! He has been telling you how he made his money. Hasn't he, now?"

"Well, yes. He took me partly into his confidence. I

congratulate you, Laura, with all my heart, for you will be a very wealthy woman."

"How strange it seems that he should have come to us in our poverty. It is all owing to you, you dear old Robert; for if he had not taken a fancy to you, he would never have come down to Elmdene and taken a fancy to some one else."

"Not at all," Robert answered, sitting down by his sister, and patting her hand affectionately. "It was a clear case of love at first sight. He was in love with you before he ever knew your name. He asked me about you the very first time I saw him."

"But tell me about his money, Bob," said his sister. "He has not told me yet, and I am so curious. How did he make it? It was not from his father; he told me that himself. His father was just a country doctor. How did he do it?"

"I am bound over to secrecy. He will tell you himself."

"Oh, but only tell me if I guess right. He had it left him by an uncle, eh? Well, by a friend? Or he took out some wonderful patent? Or he discovered a mine? Or oil? Do tell me, Robert!"

"I mustn't, really," cried her brother, laughing. "And I must not talk to you any more. You are much too sharp. I feel a responsibility about it; and, besides, I must really do some work."

"It is very unkind of you," said Laura, pouting. "But I must put my things on, for I go into Birmingham by the 1.20."

"To Birmingham?"

"Yes, I have a hundred things to order. There is everything to be got. You men forget about these details. Raffles wishes to have the wedding in little

more than a fortnight. Of course it will be very quiet,
but still one needs something."

"So early as that!" said Robert, thoughtfully. "Well,
perhaps it is better so."

"Much better, Robert. Would it not be dreadful if
Hector came back first and there was a scene? If I were
once married I should not mind. Why should I? But of
course Raffles knows nothing about him, and it would
be terrible if they came together."

"That must be avoided at any cost."

"Oh, I cannot bear even to think of it. Poor Hector!
And yet what could I do, Robert? You know that it was
only a boy and girl affair. And how could I refuse such
an offer as this? It was a duty to my family, was it not?"

"You were placed in a difficult position—very
difficult," her brother answered. "But it will be right,
and I have no doubt Hector will see it as you do. But
does Mr. Spurling know of your engagement?"

"Not a word. He was here yesterday, and talked of
Hector, but indeed I did not know how to tell him. We
are to be married by special license in Birmingham, so
really there is no reason why he should know. But now
I must hurry or I shall miss my train."

When his sister was gone Robert went up to his
studio, and having ground some colours upon his
palette he stood for some time, brush and mahlstick in
hand, in front of his big bare canvas. But how profitless
all his work seemed to him now! What object had he in
doing it? Was it to earn money? Money could be had
for the asking, or, for that matter, without the asking.
Or was it to produce a thing of beauty? But he had
artistic faults. Raffles Haw had said so, and he knew
that he was right. After all his pains the thing might not
please; and with money he could at all times buy

pictures which would please, and which would be things of beauty. What, then, was the object of his working? He could see none. He threw down his brush, and, lighting his pipe, he strolled downstairs once more.

His father was standing in front of the fire, and in no very good humour, as his red face and puckered eyes sufficed to show.

"Well, Robert," be began, "I suppose that, as usual, you have spent your morning plotting against your father?"

"What do you mean, father?"

"I mean what I say. What is it but plotting when three folk — you and she and this Raffles Haw — whisper and arrange and have meetings without a word to me about it? What do I know of your plans?"

"I cannot tell you secrets which are not my own, father."

"But I'll have a voice in the matter, for all that. Secrets or no secrets, you will find that Laura has a father, and that he is not a man to be set aside. I may have had my ups and downs in trade, but I have not quite fallen so low that I am nothing in my own family. What am I to get out of this precious marriage?"

"What should you get? Surely Laura's happiness and welfare are enough for you?"

"If this man were really fond of Laura he would show proper consideration for Laura's father. It was only yesterday that I asked him for a loan — condescended actually to ask for it — I, who have been within an ace of being Mayor of Birmingham! And he refused me point blank."

"Oh, father! How could you expose yourself to such humiliation?"

"Refused me point blank!" cried the old man excitedly. "It was against his principles, if you please. But I'll be even with him—you see if I am not. I know one or two things about him. What is it they call him at the Three Pigeons? A 'smasher'—that's the word—a coiner of false money. Why else should be have this metal sent him, and that great smokey chimney of his going all day?"

"Why, can you not leave him alone, father?" expostulated Robert. "You seem to think of nothing but his money. If he had not a penny he would still be a very kind-hearted, pleasant gentleman."

Old McIntyre burst into a hoarse laugh.

"I like to hear you preach," said he. "Without a penny, indeed! Do you think that you would dance attendance upon him if he were a poor man? Do you think that Laura would ever have looked twice at him? You know as well as I do that she is marrying him only for his money."

Robert gave a cry of dismay. There was the alchemist standing in the doorway, pale and silent, looking from one to the other of them with his searching eyes.

"I must apologize," he said coldly. "I did not mean to listen to your words. I could not help it. But I have heard them. As to you, Mr. McIntyre, I believe that you speak from your own bad heart. I will not let myself be moved by your words. In Robert I have a true friend. Laura also loves me for my own sake. You cannot shake my faith in them. But with you, Mr. McIntyre, I have nothing in common; and it is as well, perhaps, that we should both recognize the fact."

He bowed, and was gone ere either of the McIntyres could say a word.

"You see!" said Robert at last. "You have done now what you cannot undo!"

"I will be even with him!" cried the old man furiously, shaking his fist through the window at the dark slow-pacing figure. "You just wait, Robert, and see if your old dad is a man to be played with."

He had to put his ear and shoulder against the wind, and push his way forward.

XIII

A MIDNIGHT VENTURE

NOT A WORD was said to Laura when she returned as to the scene which had occurred in her absence. She was in the gayest of spirits, and prattled merrily about her purchases and her arrangements, wondering from time to time when Raffles Haw would come. As night fell, however, without any word from him, she became uneasy.

"What can be the matter that he does not come?" she said. "It is the first day since our engagement that I have not seen him."

Robert looked out through the window.

"It is a gusty night, and raining hard," he remarked. "I do not at all expect him."

"Poor Hector used to come, rain, snow, or fine. But, then, of course, he was a sailor. It was nothing to him. I hope that Raffles is not ill."

"He was quite well when I saw him this morning," answered her brother, and they relapsed into silence, while the rain pattered against the windows, and the wind screamed amid the branches of the elms outside.

Old McIntyre had sat in the corner most of the day biting his nails and glowering into the fire, with a brooding, malignant expression upon his wrinkled features. Contrary to his usual habits, he did not go to the village inn, but shuffled off early to bed without a word to his children. Laura and Robert remained chatting for some time by the fire, she talking of the thousand and one wonderful things which were to be done when she was mistress of the New Hall. There was less philanthropy in her talk when her future husband was absent, and Robert could not but remark that her carriages, her dresses, her receptions, and her travels in distant countries were the topics into which she threw all the enthusiasm which he had formerly heard her bestow upon refuge homes and labour organizations.

"I think that greys are the nicest horses," she said. "Bays are nice too, but greys are more showy. We could manage with a brougham and a landau, and perhaps a high dog-cart for Raffles. He has the coach-house full at present, but he never uses them, and I am sure that those fifty horses would all die for want of exercise, or get livers like Strasburg geese, if they waited for him to ride or drive them."

"I suppose that you will still live here?" said her brother.

"We must have a house in London as well, and run up for the season. I don't, of course, like to make suggestions now, but it will be different afterwards. I am sure that Raffles will do it if I ask him. It is all very well for him to say that he does not want any thanks or honours, but I should like to know what is the use of being a public benefactor if you are to have no return for it. I am sure that if he does only half what he talks of doing, they will make him a peer—Lord Tamfield, perhaps—and then, of course, I shall be my Lady Tamfield, and what would you think of that, Bob?" She dropped him a stately curtsey, and tossed her head in the air, as one who was born to wear a coronet.

"Father must be pensioned off," she remarked presently. "He shall have so much a year on condition that he keeps away. As to you, Bob, I don't know what we shall do for you. We shall make you President of the Royal Academy if money can do it."

It was late before they ceased building their air-castles and retired to their rooms. But Robert's brain was excited, and he could not sleep. The events of the day had been enough to shake a stronger man. There had been the revelation of the morning, the strange sights which he had witnessed in the laboratory, and the immense secret which had been confided to his keeping. Then there had been his conversation with his father in the afternoon, their disagreement, and the sudden intrusion of Raffles Haw. Finally the talk with his sister had excited his imagination, and driven sleep from his eyelids. In vain he turned and twisted in bed, or paced the floor of his chamber. He was not only awake, but abnormally awake, with every nerve highly strung, and every sense at the keenest. What was he to do to gain a little sleep? It flashed across him that there was brandy in the decanter downstairs, and that a glass might act as a sedative.

He had opened the door of his room, when suddenly his ear caught the sound of slow and stealthy footsteps upon the stairs. His own lamp was unlit, but a dim glimmer came from a moving taper, and a long black shadow travelled down the wall. He stood motionless, listening intently. The steps were in the hall now, and he heard a gentle creaking as the key was cautiously turned in the door. The next instant there came a gust of cold air, the taper was extinguished, and a sharp snap announced that the door had been closed from without.

Robert stood astonished. Who could this night wanderer be? It must be his father. But what errand could take him out at three in the morning? And such a morning, too! With every blast of the wind the rain beat up against his chamber-window as though it would drive it in. The glass rattled in the frames, and the tree outside creaked and groaned as its great branches were tossed about by the gale. What could draw any man forth upon such a night?

Hurriedly Robert struck a match and lit his lamp. His father's room was opposite his own, and the door was ajar. He pushed it open and looked about him. It was empty. The bed had not even been lain upon. The single chair stood by the window, and there the old man must have sat since he left them. There was no book, no paper, no means by which he could have amused himself, nothing but a razor-strop lying on the window-sill.

A feeling of impending misfortune struck cold to Robert's heart. There was some ill-meaning in this journey of his father's. He thought of his brooding of yesterday, his scowling face, his bitter threats. Yes, there was some mischief underlying it. But perhaps he might even now be in time to prevent it. There was no use calling Laura. She could be no help in the matter. He hurriedly threw on his clothes, muffled himself in his topcoat, and, seizing his hat and stick, he set off after his father.

As he came out into the village street the wind whirled down it, so that he had to put his ear and shoulder against it, and push his way forward. It was better, however, when he turned into the lane. The high bank and the hedge sheltered him upon one side. The road, however, was deep in mud, and the rain fell in a steady swish. Not a soul was to be seen, but he needed to make no inquiries, for he knew whither his father had gone as certainly as though he had seen him.

The iron side gate of the Avenue was half open, and Robert stumbled his way up the gravelled drive amid the dripping fir-trees. What could his father's intention be when he reached the Hall? Was it merely that he wished to spy and prowl, or did he intend to call up the master and enter into some discussion as to his wrongs? Or was it possible that some blacker and more sinister design lay beneath his strange doings? Robert thought suddenly of the razor-strop, and gasped with horror. What had the old man been doing with that? He quickened his pace to a run, and hurried on until he found himself at the door of the Hall.

Thank God! all was quiet there. He stood by the big silent door and listened intently. There was nothing to be heard save the wind and the rain. Where, then, could his father be? If he wished to enter the Hall he would not attempt to do so by one of the windows, for had he not been present when Raffles Haw had shown them the precautions which he had taken? But then a sudden thought struck Robert. There was one window which was left unguarded. Haw had been imprudent enough to tell them so. It was the middle window of the laboratory. If he remembered it so clearly, of course his father would remember it too. There was the point of danger.

The moment that he had come round the corner of the building he found that his surmise had been correct. An electric lamp burned in the laboratory, and the silver squares of the three large windows stood out clear and bright in the darkness. The centre one had been thrown open, and, even as he gazed, Robert saw a dark monkey-like figure spring up on to the sill, and vanish into the room beyond. For a moment only it outlined itself against the brilliant light beyond, but in that moment Robert had space to see that it was indeed his father. On tiptoe he crossed the intervening space, and peeped in through the open window. It was a singular spectacle which met his eyes.

There stood upon the glass table some half-dozen large ingots of gold, which had been made the night before, but which had not been removed to the treasure-house. On these the old man had thrown himself, as one who enters into his rightful inheritance. He lay across the table, his arms clasping the bars of gold, his cheek pressed against them, crooning and muttering to himself. Under the clear, still light, amid the giant wheels and strange engines, that one little dark figure clutching and clinging to the ingots had in it something both weird and piteous.

For five minutes or more Robert stood in the darkness amid the rain, looking in at this strange sight, while his father hardly moved save to cuddle closer to the gold, and to pat it with his thin hands. Robert was still uncertain what he should do, when his eyes wandered from the central figure and fell on something else which made him give a little cry of astonishment — a cry which was drowned amid the howling of the gale.

Raffles Haw was standing in the corner of the room. Where he had come from Robert could not say, but he was certain that he had not been there when he first looked in. He stood silent, wrapped in some long, dark dressing-gown, his arms folded, and a bitter smile upon his pale face. Old McIntyre seemed to see him at almost the same moment, for he snarled out an oath, and clutched still closer at his treasure, looking slantwise at the master of the house with furtive, treacherous eyes.

"And it has really come to this!" said Haw at last, taking a step forward. "You have actually fallen so low, Mr. McIntyre, as to steal into my house at night like a common burglar. You knew that this window was unguarded. I remember telling you as much. But I did not tell you what other means I had adopted by which I might be warned if knaves made an entrance. But that you should have come! You!"

The old gunmaker made no attempt to justify himself, but he muttered some few hoarse words, and continued to cling to the treasure.

"I love your daughter," said Raffles Haw, "and for her sake I will not expose you. Your hideous and infamous secret shall be safe with me. No ear shall hear what has happened this night. I will not, as I might, arouse my servants and send for the police. But you must leave my house without further words. I have nothing more to say to you. Go as you have come."

He took a step forward, and held out his hand as if to detach the old man's grasp from the golden bars. The other thrust his hand into the breast of his coat, and with a shrill scream of rage flung himself upon the alchemist. So sudden and so fierce was the movement that Haw had no time for defense. A bony hand gripped him by the throat, and the blade of a razor flashed in the air. Fortunately, as it fell, the weapon struck against one of the many wires which spanned the room, and flying out of the old man's grasp, tinkled upon the stone floor. But, though disarmed, he was still dangerous. With a horrible silent energy he pushed Haw back and back until, coming to a bench, they both fell over it, McIntyre remaining uppermost. His other hand was on the alchemist's throat, and it might have fared ill with him had Robert not climbed through the window and dragged his father off from him. With the aid of Haw, he pinned the old man down, and passed a long cravat around his arms. It was terrible to look at him, for his face was convulsed, his eyes bulging from his head, and his lips white with foam.

Haw leaned against the glass table panting, with his hand to his side.

"You here, Robert?" he gasped. "Is it not horrible? How did you come?"

"I followed him. I heard him go out."

"He would have robbed me. And he would have murdered me. But he is mad — stark, staring mad!"

There could be no doubt of it. Old McIntyre was sitting up now, and burst suddenly into a hoarse peal of laughter, rocking himself backwards and forwards, and looking up at them with little twinkling, cunning eyes. It was clear to both of them that his mind, weakened by long brooding over the one idea, had now at last become that of a monomaniac. His horrid causeless mirth was more terrible even than his fury.

"What shall we do with him?" asked Haw. "We cannot take him back to Elmdene. It would be a terrible shock to Laura."

"We could have doctors to certify in the morning. Could we not keep him here until then? If we take him back, some one will meet us, and there will be a scandal."

"I know. We will take him to one of the padded rooms, where he can neither hurt himself nor anyone else. I am somewhat shaken myself. But I am better now. Do you take one arm, and I will take the other."

Half-leading and half-dragging him they managed between them to convey the old gunmaker away from the scene of his disaster, and to lodge him for the night in a place of safety. At five in the morning Robert had started in the gig to make the medical arrangements, while Raffles Haw paced his palatial house with a troubled face and a sad heart.

"Hector!" she gasped.

XIV

The Spread of the Blight

I T MAY BE that Laura did not look upon the removal
of her father as an unmixed misfortune. Nothing
was said to her as to the manner of the old man's
seizure, but Robert informed her at breakfast that he
had thought it best, acting under medical advice, to
place him for a time under some restraint. She had
herself frequently remarked upon the growing eccen-
tricity of his manner, so that the announcement could
have been no great surprise to her. It is certain that it
did not diminish her appetite for the coffee and the
scrambled eggs, nor prevent her from chatting a good
deal about her approaching wedding.

But it was very different with Raffles Haw. The
incident had shocked him to his inmost soul. He had
often feared lest his money should do indirect evil, but
here were crime and madness arising before his very
eyes from its influence. In vain he tried to choke down
his feelings, and to persuade himself that this attack of
old McIntyre's was something which came of itself—
something which had no connection with himself or his
wealth. He remembered the man as he had first met
him, garrulous, foolish, but with no obvious vices. He
recalled the change which, week by week, had come
over him—his greedy eye, his furtive manner, his hints

and innuendoes, ending only the day before in a positive demand for money. It was too certain that there was a chain of events there leading direct to the horrible encounter in the laboratory. His money had cast a blight where he had hoped to shed a blessing.

Mr. Spurling, the vicar, was up shortly after breakfast, some rumour of evil having come to his ears. It was good for Haw to talk with him, for the fresh breezy manner of the old clergyman was a corrective to his own sombre and introspective mood.

"Prut, tut!" said he. "This is very bad—very bad indeed! Mind unhinged, you say, and not likely to get over it! Dear, dear! I have noticed a change in him these last few weeks. He looked like a man who had something upon his mind. And how is Mr. Robert McIntyre?"

"He is very well. He was with me this morning when his father had this attack."

"Ha! There is a change in that young man. I observe an alteration in him. You will forgive me, Mr. Raffles Haw, if I say a few serious words of advice to you. Apart from my spiritual functions I am old enough to be your father. You are a very wealthy man, and you have used your wealth nobly—yes, sir, nobly. I do not think that there is a man in a thousand who would have done as well. But don't you think sometimes that it has a dangerous influence upon those who are around you?"

"I have sometimes feared so."

"We may pass over old Mr. McIntyre. It would hardly be just, perhaps, to mention him in this connection. But there is Robert. He used to take such an interest in his profession. He was so keen about art. If you met him, the first words he said were usually some reference to his plans, or the progress he was making in his latest picture. He was ambitious, pushing, self-reliant. Now he does nothing. I know for a fact that it is two months since he put brush to canvas. He has turned from a student into an idler, and, what is worse, I fear into a parasite. You will forgive me for speaking so plainly?"

Raffles Haw said nothing, but he threw out his hands with a gesture of pain.

"And then there is something to be said about the country folk," said the vicar. "Your kindness has been, perhaps, a little indiscriminate there. They don't seem to be as helpful or as self-reliant as they used. There was old Blaxton, whose cowhouse roof was blown off the other day. He used to be a man who was full of energy and resource. Three months ago he would have got a ladder and had that roof on again in two days' work. But now he must sit down, and wring his hands, and write letters, because he knew that it would come to your ears, and that you would make it good. There's old Ellary, too! Well, of course he was always poor, but at least he did something, and so kept himself out of mischief. Not a stroke will he do now, but smokes and talks scandal from morning to night. And the worst of it is, that it not only hurts those who have had your help, but it unsettles those who have not. They all have an injured, surly feeling as if other folk were getting what they had an equal right to. It has really come to such a pitch that I thought it was a duty to speak to you about it. Well, it is a new experience to me. I have often had to reprove my parishioners for not being charitable enough, but it is very strange to find one who is too charitable. It is a noble error."

"I thank you very much for letting me know about

it," answered Raffles Haw, as he shook the good old clergyman's hand. "I shall certainly reconsider my conduct in that respect."

He kept a rigid and unmoved face until his visitor had gone, and then retiring to his own little room, he threw himself upon the bed and burst out sobbing with his face buried in the pillow. Of all men in England, this, the richest, was on that day the most miserable. How could he use this great power which he held? Every blessing which he tried to give turned into a curse. His intentions were so good, and yet the results were so terrible. It was as if he had some foul leprosy of the mind which all caught who were exposed to his influence. His charity, so well meant, so carefully bestowed, had yet poisoned the whole country side. And if in small things his results were so evil, how could he tell that they would be better in the larger plans which he had formed? If he could not pay the debts of a simple yokel without disturbing the great laws of cause and effect which lie at the base of all things, what could he hope for when he came to fill the treasury of nations, to interfere with the complex conditions of trade, or to provide for great masses of the population? He drew back with horror as he dimly saw that vast problems faced him in which he might make errors which all his money could not repair. The way of Providence was the straight way. Yet he, a half-blind creature, must needs push in and strive to alter and correct it. Would he be a benefactor? Might he not rather prove to be the greatest malefactor that the world had seen?

But soon a calmer mood came upon him, and he rose and bathed his flushed face and fevered brow. After all, was not there a field where all were agreed that money might be well spent? It was not the way of nature, but rather the way of man which he would alter. It was not Providence that had ordained that folk should live half-starved and overcrowded in dreary slums. That was the result of artificial conditions, and it might well be healed by artificial means. Why should not his plans be successful after all, and the world better for his discovery? Then again, it was not the truth that he cast a blight on those with whom he was brought in contact. There was Laura; who knew more of him than she did, and yet how good and sweet and true she was! She at least had lost nothing through knowing him. He would go down and see her. It would be soothing to hear her voice, and to turn to her for words of sympathy in this his hour of darkness.

The storm had died away, but a soft wind was blowing, and the smack of the coming spring was in the air. He drew in the aromatic scent of the fir-trees as he passed down the curving drive. Before him lay the long sloping country side, all dotted over with the farm-steads and little red cottages, with the morning sun striking slantwise upon their grey roofs and glimmering windows. His heart yearned over all these people with their manifold troubles, their little sordid miseries, their strivings and hopings and petty soul-killing cares. How could he get at them? How could he manage to lift the burden from them, and yet not hinder them in their life aim? For more and more could he see that all refinement is through sorrow, and that the life which does not refine is the life without an aim.

Laura was alone in the sitting-room at Elmdene, for Robert had gone out to make some final arrangements about his father. She sprang up as her lover entered, and ran forward with a pretty girlish gesture to greet him.

"Oh, Raffles!" she cried, "I knew that you would come. Is it not dreadful about papa?"

"You must not fret, dearest," he answered gently. "It may not prove to be so very grave after all."

"But it all happened before I was stirring. I knew nothing about it until breakfast-time. They must have gone up to the Hall very early."

"Yes, they did come up rather early."

"What is the matter with you, Raffles?" cried Laura, looking up into his face. "You look so sad and weary!"

"I have been a little in the blues. The fact is, Laura, that I have had a long talk with Mr. Spurling this morning."

The girl started, and turned white to the lips. A long talk with Mr. Spurling! Did that mean that he had learned her secret?

"Well?" she gasped.

"He tells me that my charity has done more harm than good, and in fact, that I have had an evil influence upon every one whom I have come near. He said it in the most delicate way, but that was really what it amounted to."

"Oh, is that all?" said Laura, with a long sigh of relief. "You must not think of minding what Mr. Spurling says. Why, it is absurd on the face of it! Everybody knows that there are dozens of men all over the country who would have been ruined and turned out of their houses if you had not stood their friend. How could they be the worse for having known you? I wonder that Mr. Spurling can talk such nonsense!"

"How is Robert's picture getting on?"

"Oh, he has a lazy fit on him. He has not touched it for ever so long. But why do you ask that? You have that furrow on your brow again. Put it away, sir!"

She smoothed it away with her little white hand.

"Well, at any rate, I don't think that quite everybody is the worse," said he, looking down at her. "There is one, at least, who is beyond taint, one who is good, and pure, and true, and who would love me as well if I were a poor clerk struggling for a livelihood. You would, would you not, Laura?"

"You foolish boy! of course I would."

"And yet how strange it is that it should be so. That you, who are the only woman whom I have ever loved, should be the only one in whom I also have raised an affection which is free from greed or interest. I wonder whether you may not have been sent by Providence simply to restore my confidence in the world. How barren a place would it not be if it were not for woman's love! When all seemed black around me this morning, I tell you, Laura, that I seemed to turn to you and to your love as the one thing on earth upon which I could rely. All else seemed shifting, unstable, influenced by this or that base consideration. In you, and you only, could I trust."

"And I in you, dear Raffles! I never knew what love was until I met you."

She took a step towards him, her hands advanced, love shining in her features, when in an instant Raffles saw the colour struck from her face, and a staring horror spring into her eyes. Her blanched and rigid face was turned towards the open door, while he, standing partly behind it, could not see what it was that had so moved her.

"Hector!" she gasped, with dry lips.

A quick step in the hall, and a slim, weather-tanned young man sprang forward into the room, and caught her up in his arms as if she had been a feather.

"You darling!" he said; "I knew that I would surprise you. I came right up from Plymouth by the night train. And I have long leave, and plenty of time to get married. Isn't it jolly, dear Laura?"

He pirouetted round with her in the exuberance of his delight. As he spun round, however, his eyes fell suddenly upon the pale and silent stranger who stood by the door. Hector blushed furiously, and made an awkward sailor bow, standing with Laura's cold and unresponsive hand still clasped in his.

"Very sorry, sir—didn't see you," he said. "You'll excuse my going on in this mad sort of way, but if you had served you would know what it is to get away from quarter-deck manners, and to be a free man. Miss McIntyre will tell you that we have known each other since we were children, and as we are to be married in, I hope, a month at the latest, we understand each other pretty well."

Raffles Haw stood cold and motionless. He was stunned, benumbed, by what he saw and heard. Laura drew away from Hector, and tried to free her hand from his grasp.

"Didn't you get my letter at Gibraltar?" she asked.

"Never went to Gibraltar. Were ordered home by wire from Madeira. Those chaps at the Admiralty never know their own minds for two hours together. But what matter about a letter, Laura, so long as I can see you and speak with you? You have not introduced me to your friend here."

"One word, sir," cried Raffles Haw in a quivering voice. "Do I entirely understand you? Let me be sure that there is no mistake. You say that you are engaged to be married to Miss McIntyre?"

"Of course I am. I've just come back from a four

months' cruise, and I am going to be married before I drag my anchor again."

"Four months!" gasped Haw. "Why, it is just four months since I came here. And one last question, sir. Does Robert McIntyre know of your engagement?"

"Does Bob know? Of course he knows. Why, it was to his care I left Laura when I started. But what is the meaning of all this? What is the matter with you, Laura? Why are you so white and silent? And—hallo! Hold up, sir! The man is fainting!"

"It is all right!" gasped Haw, steadying himself against the edge of the door.

He was as white as paper, and his hand was pressed close to his side as though some sudden pain had shot through him. For a moment he tottered there like a stricken man, and then, with a hoarse cry, he turned and fled out through the open door.

"Poor devil!" said Hector, gazing in amazement after him. "He seems hard hit anyhow. But what is the meaning of all this, Laura?"

His face had darkened, and his mouth had set.

She had not said a word, but had stood with a face like a mask looking blankly in front of her. Now she tore herself away from him, and, casting herself down with her face buried in the cushion of the sofa, she burst into a passion of sobbing.

"It means that you have ruined me," she cried. "That you have ruined—ruined—ruined me! Could you not leave us alone? Why must you come at the last moment? A few more days, and we were safe. And you never had my letter."

"And what was in your letter, then?" he asked coldly, standing with his arms folded, looking down at her.

"It was to tell you that I released you. I love Raffles Haw, and I was to have been his wife. And now it is all gone. Oh, Hector, I hate you, and I shall always hate you as long as I live, for you have stepped between me and the only good fortune that ever came to me. Leave me alone, and I hope that you will never cross our threshold again."

"Is that your last word, Laura?"

"The last that I shall ever speak to you."

"Then, good-bye. I shall see the Dad, and go straight back to Plymouth." He waited an instant, in hopes of an answer, and then walked sadly from the room.

XV

THE GREATER SECRET

IT was late that night that a startled knocking came at the door of Elmdene. Laura had been in her room all day, and Robert was moodily smoking his pipe by the fire, when this harsh and sudden summons broke in upon his thoughts. There in the porch was Jones, the stout head-butler of the Hall, hatless, scared, with the raindrops shining in the lamp-light upon his smooth, bald head.

"If you please, Mr. McIntyre, sir, would it trouble you to step up to the Hall?" he cried. "We are all frightened, sir, about master."

Robert caught up his hat and started at a run, the frightened butler trotting heavily beside him. It had been a day of excitement and disaster. The young artist's heart was heavy within him, and the shadow of some crowning trouble seemed to have fallen upon his soul.

"What is the matter with your master, then?" he asked, as he slowed down into a walk.

"We don't know, sir; but we can't get an answer when we knock at the laboratory door. Yet he's there, for it's locked on the inside. It has given us all a scare, sir, that, and his goin's-on during the day."

"His goings-on?"

"Yes, sir; for he came back this morning like a man demented, a-talkin' to himself, and with his eyes starin' so that it was dreadful to look at the poor dear gentleman. Then he walked about the passages a long time, and he wouldn't so much as look at his luncheon, but he went into the museum, and gathered all his jewels and things, and carried them into the laboratory. We don't know what he's done since then, sir, but his furnace has been a-roarin', and his big chimney spoutin' smoke like a Birmingham factory. When night came we could see his figure against the light, a-workin' and a-heavin' like a man possessed. No dinner would he have, but work, and work, and work. Now it's all quiet, and the furnace cold, and no smoke from above, but we can't get no answer from him, sir, so we are scared, and Miller has gone for the police, and I came away for you."

They reached the Hall as the butler finished his explanation, and there outside the laboratory door stood the little knot of footmen and ostlers, while the village policeman, who had just arrived, was holding his bull's-eye to the keyhole, and endeavouring to peep through.

"The key is half-turned," he said. "I can't see nothing except just the light."

"Here's Mr. McIntyre," cried half-a-dozen voices, as Robert came forward.

"We'll have to beat the door in, sir," said the policeman. "We can't get any sort of answer, and there's something wrong."

Twice and thrice they threw their united weights against it until at last with a sharp snap the lock broke, and they crowded into the narrow passage. The inner door was ajar, and the laboratory lay before them.

In the centre was an enormous heap of fluffy grey ash, reaching up half-way to the ceiling. Beside it was another heap, much smaller, of some brilliant scintillating dust, which shimmered brightly in the rays of the electric light. All round was a bewildering chaos of broken jars, shattered bottles, cracked machinery, and tangled wires, all bent and draggled. And there in the midst of this universal ruin, leaning back in his chair with his hands clasped upon his lap, and the easy pose of one who rests after hard work safely carried through, sat Raffles Haw, the master of the house, and the richest of mankind, with the pallor of death upon his face. So easily he sat and so naturally, with such a serene expression upon his features, that it was not until they raised him, and touched his cold and rigid limbs, that they could realize that he had indeed passed away.

Reverently and slowly they bore him to his room, for he was beloved by all who had served him. Robert alone lingered with the policeman in the laboratory. Like a man in a dream he wandered about, marvelling at the universal destruction. A large broad-headed hammer lay upon the ground, and with this Haw had apparently set himself to destroy all his apparatus, having first used his electrical machines to reduce to protyle all the stock of gold which he had accumulated. The treasure-room which had so dazzled Robert consisted now of merely four bare walls, while the gleaming dust upon the floor proclaimed the fate of that magnificent collection of gems which had alone amounted to a royal fortune. Of all the machinery no single piece remained intact, and even the glass table was shattered into three pieces. Strenuously earnest must have been the work which Raffles Haw had done that day.

And suddenly Robert thought of the secret which had been treasured in the casket within the iron-clamped box. It was to tell him the one last essential link which would make his knowledge of the process complete. Was it still there? Thrilling all over, he opened the great chest, and drew out the ivory box. It was locked, but the key was in it. He turned it and threw open the lid. There was a white slip of paper with his own name written upon it. With trembling fingers he unfolded it. Was he the heir to the riches of El Dorado, or was he destined to be a poor struggling artist? The note was dated that very evening, and ran in this way: —

"MY DEAR ROBERT, — My secret shall never be used again. I cannot tell you how I thank Heaven that I did not entirely confide it to you, for I should have been handing over an inheritance of misery both to yourself and others. For myself I have hardly had a happy moment since I discovered it. This I could have borne, but, alas! the only effect of my attempts has been to turn workers into idlers, contented men into greedy parasites, and, worst of all, true, pure women into deceivers and hypocrites. If this is the effect of my interference on a small scale, I cannot hope for anything better were I to carry out the plans which we have so often discussed. The schemes of my life have all turned to nothing. For myself, you shall never see me again. I shall go back to the student life from which I emerged. There, at least, if I can do little good, I can do no harm. It is my wish that such valuables as remain in the Hall should be sold, and the proceeds divided amidst all the charities of Birmingham. I shall leave to-night if I am well enough, but I have been much troubled all day by a stabbing pain in my side. It is as if wealth were as bad for health as it is for peace of mind. Good-bye, Robert, and may you never have as sad a heart as I have to-night. — Yours very truly,

                                        "RAFFLES HAW."

"Was it suicide, sir? Was it suicide?" broke in the policeman as Robert put the note in his pocket.

"No," he answered; "I think it was a broken heart."

And so the wonders of the New Hall were all dismantled, the carvings and the gold, the books and the pictures, and many a struggling man or woman who had heard nothing of Raffles Haw during his life had cause to bless him after his death. The house has been bought by a company now, who have turned it into a hydropathic establishment, and of all the folk who frequent it in search of health or of pleasure there are few who know the strange story which is connected with it.

The blight which Haw's wealth cast around it seemed to last even after his death. Old McIntyre still raves in the County Lunatic Asylum, and treasures up old scraps of wood and metal under the impression that they are all ingots of gold. Robert McIntyre is a moody and irritable man, for ever pursuing a quest which will always evade him. His art is forgotten, and he spends his whole small income upon chemical and electrical appliances, with which he vainly seeks to rediscover that one hidden link. His sister keeps house for him, a silent and brooding woman, still queenly and beautiful, but of a bitter, dissatisfied mind. Of late, however, she has devoted herself to charity, and has been of so much help to Mr. Spurling's new curate that it is thought that he may be tempted to secure her assistance for ever. So runs the gossip of the village, and in small places such gossip is seldom wrong. As to Hector Spurling, he is still in her Majesty's service, and seems inclined to abide by his father's wise advice, that he should not think of marrying until he was a Commander. It is

possible that of all who were brought within the spell of
Raffles Haw he was the only one who had occasion to
bless it.

AFTERWORD

"I DARE SAY that when you are famous they will be of value as specimens of your early manner." So says Raffles Haw of young Robert McIntyre's canvases in the fifth chapter of *The Doings of Raffles Haw.* So one might have spoken to Sir Arthur Conan Doyle about *Raffles Haw* itself. Perhaps Raffles's assessment of Robert's pictures is Doyle's own apt opinion of this novel: "But your drawing, if you will excuse my saying so, is just a little crude, and your colouring perhaps a trifle thin."

It is not an especially memorable work. I confess that, when I reread it for this Afterword, it was for the first time since the mid-1930s. As a collector of material relating to Sherlock Holmes, I have on my shelves six different editions of *The Doings of Raffles Haw,* but only because the copies published in the United States have included two or more of the cases from the Watsonian canon. But I can report that this rereading was a pleasurable experience, for Conan Doyle, when writing fiction, is almost always exciting. He was a master of characterization and was one of the most absorbing storytellers of all time. Alas, we have too few of these raconteurs writing today.

The Doings of Raffles Haw is a moral tale, a parable. One would expect Arthur Conan Doyle, especially at the early age of thirty-two, to moralize. His upbringing was in a traditional Irish-Catholic home, steeped in the admiration of the honour of ancestors who lived and worked for God and their people. He was instructed by his mother with great firmness of purpose to be, in effect, a knight, devoted to right conduct and to defend against evil, and to assume a responsibility for others, especially those less fortunate, poorer, or uneducated. In following Doyle's long career, one can observe that he always kept this conviction, almost a compulsion, to defend that in which he believed, come what may. This may account for the single-minded, unwavering defense of Spiritualism that dominated his later years.

In this tale, Doyle seems to demonstrate his belief that any tampering with the *status quo* of society is ill-advised. This status is the result of the work of centuries, work done by great and noble Englishmen who built a well-structured society to which he, Doyle, fully subscribes. One who attempts to change all this will find failure. Better to leave it to the politicians, to the church, to organized charity, and to natural processes. Do not take into your hands the problems of the masses, however well-intentioned you may be, or fate will deal with you as it did with poor Haw.

It is assumed by the author, and he assumes that it will be so with the reader, that the lower classes react the way they do in Tamfield, that greed is dominant and that it will change persons and their plans — at once and completely — that a person is ill-advised to try on his own to help others, that one is powerless in such a structured society, that what is must be, for, after all, Doyle's own class believe this.

Unlike so many of Doyle's literary creations, this one took no new departure. Rather, in style, in character, and in the moral to be drawn from the plot, it is typical of so many other stories of these late Victorian times. It is from the first predictable, full of the stereotyped Victorian reactions and manners — prudishness, feelings of class exclusivity, stiffness in personal response. It would be but another forgotten, forgettable, dull period piece, dealing with two-dimensional people, were it not for the genius of the writer as a storyteller and as a creator of character.

One delight is Conan Doyle's recurring ability to predict the future. For Sherlock Holmes, he virtually invented the concept of scientific crime detection — so much so that, in the early days before textbooks could be prepared, many Continental police forces used the Holmes stories to school their men in the subject. Later, Doyle predicted the dangers of submarine warfare against British shipping and originated the ideas of life jackets for sailors and steel battle helmets for the soldiers in the trenches of World War I. The all-electric house in *The Doings of Raffles Haw,* with its self-opening doors, beverage dispensers, automatic burglar alarms, and much more, should come as no surprise.

And once again he has created, even in such short space, memorable characters — characters such as Laura and Robert and old Mr. McIntyre, the vicar, and Hector the sailor swain. They are memorable and believable — excluding, however, Mr. Raffles Haw himself, who is stiff cardboard throughout, used only as a means to point up the serious moral issue.

Very little has been written about this obscure novel from a critical or biographical standpoint. The word "feeble" crops up in more than one of Doyle's biographers' remarks, all of which are passing ones. Several biographies, and notably the best of them all, by John

Dickson Carr, do not mention *Raffles Haw* at all. Reviews at the time were few, and mixed—after July 1891, the appearance of the Sherlock Holmes stories in the *Strand* magazine had catapulted Doyle to fame and fortune, but it would still be some years before he found favour with the "serious" literary critics. He in his own *Memories and Adventures* writes: "I also wrote one short book, *The Doings of Raffles Haw,* not a very notable achievement, by which I was able to pay my current expenses."

It appears that the whole purpose of writing this book may not have been so much to moralize about the evils of riches as to secure the funds necessary to pay for an impulsive trip to Vienna to study the diseases of the eye, for he was yet a practising physician at this time, even after moving to London from his "busy though ill-paying" practice in the suburbs of Portsmouth, and he had determined to take up ophthalmology as his specialty. It is recorded in his diary under the date of February 3 (1891): "Raffles Haw, £150."

And from an April entry in the same year, we learn that he received £40 for the American serial rights—yet notable Doyle scholars and researchers, particularly the late Jay Finley Christ, have been unable to locate any periodical appearance of this tale.

It is of interest that current prices for a single copy of the first edition of this book are over the £40 that Doyle received for the American rights. And the true first edition of *The Doings of Raffles Haw* is the American one, for it was published late in 1891 and the British edition not until 1892.

One more facet of Conan Doyle's great charm and ability as a writer was his creation of interesting and memorable names. Graham Greene, in his precisely-written introduction to the Murray/Cape edition of *The Sign of Four,* declares that Doyle's mastery of names is "perhaps equalled only by Dickens." Names such as Raffles Haw. It is generally considered a fact that, years later, when Doyle's brother-in-law E. W. Hornung wrote about the charming and successful gentleman crook whom he named Raffles, he borrowed the name from A.C.D.

I approve of the reprinting of this barely-known work. "Feeble" it may be, but it still provides a good read, and certainly it must have some importance in the development of the science-fiction genre. It is still my opinion that any fiction written by Doyle—no, anything at all written by Doyle other than the Spiritualist stuff—gives pleasure and is always worth the effort to peruse.

JOHN BENNETT SHAW

August 1980